I thought I had learne
wrong...

It had gotten much colder in the past few weeks, and the snow was getting deeper. I shivered as flakes of snow swirled around me. The sidewalk in front of me was dark as I made my way to the mall that was another block away, my breath visible in the cold air.

The wind wreaked havoc with my hearing aids, blocking out every sound around me. It drove me nuts since it was irritating and uncomfortably loud. I shivered as another blast of cold air slammed me in my face, forcing me to turn my head away from it.

At that moment, I could swear I heard a whistle or someone yelling at me. I looked up into the fierce wind, squinting my eyes but not seeing anyone in front of me. Strange, I thought. Maybe it's my imagination. I continued on, staggering slightly from the wind.

I heard it again, this time mixed with voices that were loud but didn't make any sense. Then, I saw their shadow behind me. Gulping back the fear that was rising through my body, I picked up the pace, more afraid than ever. Suddenly, a big shove across my back sent me stumbling awkwardly and I frantically tried to regain my balance. Someone grabbed my shoulder and spun me around.

There was something different about Jessie. She struggled to fit in at school, surrounded by a web of lies and deceit...until she met Ethan.

Based on a true story, the novel "Sway" is about a hearing impaired teenager named Jessie who tries her best to blend in at school. Every day proves to be a test of her resolve when she is constantly plagued by the ruthless pranks of her classmates who are determined to make her life miserable. When a handsome stranger arrives in the nick of time, Jessie wonders if he is too good to be true. Is Ethan's attention genuine, or will he betray her trust, too?

KUDOS for *Sway*

Twitter: "Read *Sway* and loved it. I cried for the good first half of it."

C. S.: "After I started it, I was compelled to finish reading it...I finally finished it at 1:30 am. I enjoyed reading the book and hope you have a sequel to it."

www.kobobooks.com: "This is a great book! Read it, definitely!"

Woven into the story is a sweet little romance that adds not only warmth, but vindication. I was thrilled to see Jessie get the hunk—the hunk with rich parents, no less. Ethan is charming and sees Jessie for what she is, not what she isn't. If you are looking for a story that will make you walk a mile in someone else's shoes, warm your heart, and give you a greater appreciation for what you have, you can't go wrong with *Sway*. – *Taylor, Reviewer*

I thought *Sway* was fascinating. While it was again about high school, which I hated and have no desire to revisit, it was different. This book was high school as seen through the eyes of a hearing-impaired teenager...I can't even comprehend how hard it must have been for her...*Sway* is heartwarming and touching, and although Jessie forgives her friends, I am still angry at them. The story gives you a glimpse into a world that everyone should spend a little time in. Maybe then we could learn compassion. – *Regan, Reviewer*

SWAY HAS CONSISTENTLY BEEN A TOP-50 BESTSELLER AT www.kobobooks.com!

Sway

by

Jennifer Gibson

A BLACK OPAL BOOKS PUBLICATION

GENRE: YA/ROMANCE

SWAY
Copyright © 2012 by Jennifer Gibson
Cover Design by Jennifer Gibson
All cover art copyright © 2012
All Rights Reserved
PRINT ISBN: 978-1-937329-59-4

First Publication: AUGUST 2012

Published by Black Opal Books **http://www.blackopalbooks.com**

ACKNOWLEDGMENTS

As a child, I grew up surrounded by an abundance of books which allowed my mind to take a much needed break from school and everyday life. It gave me the freedom to roam through the creative and wonderful worlds penned by imaginative authors. I owe my parents a debt of gratitude for providing these delightful novels and giving me an opportunity to fall in love with them.

A big thank you goes to my Mom for her extensive proofreading and editing skills and for actively encouraging me to consider publishing this novel.

I must extend my most gracious thanks to my publisher Black Opal Books and my extraordinary editors, Susan, Faith, and Lauri for their enthusiastic support. You made a seemingly impossible dream come miraculously true. Now if only unicorns were real...

Kudos to all of my test readers for giving me a helping hand!

Arigato.

Author's Notes

Did you know that there are over 20 million people in North America that have some form of hearing loss?

It's a common misconception that hearing impairment affects the elderly. Unfortunately this stigma is not accurate since it can happen to anyone at any age, from newborns to children and young adults.

Chances are that you already know someone that wears hearing aids or has difficulty hearing. It could be someone at school, a neighbor down the street, co-worker, or even a player on your team. They are just like you, the only difference is that the world is a bit quieter to them.

Being hard of hearing makes it very difficult to be a part of the society and unfortunately, is an isolating disability that can have a debilitating effect on a person's life. Helen Keller said it best: "Blindness cuts us off from things, but deafness cuts us off from people."

CHAPTER 1

Silver Lining

Everything seemed to go wrong from the moment I woke up this morning. First it was my missing gym shorts, then it was not being able to find the essay that was due today. I frantically scarfed down my breakfast to make it to the bus on time and ran down the long lane, barely making it as I awkwardly lugged my overflowing backpack. By the time I reached the doorway at school, my mind was already scattered. It felt like an angry storm was surging inside my head.

I searched through my locker, grabbed the heavy books and binder I needed for my next class, tossed them into my backpack, pulled out my pencil case from the top shelf in one hand, and with my other hand slammed the locker shut. I was in the process of pushing the lock closed when suddenly my pencil case fell to the floor. I sighed, frustrated. It had not been an easy day despite the cheerful weather outside. Even the birds twittered madly as if they were trying to drive me insane.

My fingers reached downwards, just barely grasping the pencil case when it suddenly flew out of my hands. I heard laughter behind me as I glanced up to see Patricia kick it across the smooth floor and snatch it up, gleefully tossing it back and forth with Mitchell.

I groaned. Those two delinquents were the bane of my existence and I really didn't need this additional aggravation today.

"Oh come on! Can you possibly get any more childish?" I threw up my hands in frustration, my temper simmering as I watched them toss it to each other, laughing.

"What? You don't wanna play with us?" Patricia snickered scornfully. She knew that she drove me nuts and took pleasure in tormenting me at every possible opportunity. She was one of the meanest girls I had encountered at this school.

Oh, there were others equally as vile but they were more cunning, skillful with their antics. Patricia was a constant thorn in my side and this was not a good day for her to poke it deeper.

I nearly growled. "No, now please give it back to me." Rage was building in me, bubbling hot in my chest. "I need it for class."

"You really need it?" she said in mock innocence but her lips curling over her teeth revealed her sinister intentions.

"Well then, go get it!"

I could only stare in shock as she threw it into the boy's washroom. Stunned, I felt rooted to the floor. My thoughts scrambled madly to catch up with the scene in front of me.

The bell rang, breaking into my thoughts. I numbly watched Patricia and Mitchell pivot around and run down the hall toward their classroom laughing as they went, giving each other high fives.

I breathed in and out several times, trying to gather my wits. I told myself to move to the washroom and look for it. *How hard could it be?* I thought. *Oh for the love of Pete, I'm acting ridiculous. Just get the damn thing or you'll be late for class!*

I strolled over to the boys' washroom, shoved the door open and yelled, "Hello? Anyone in there?" When there was no response, I moved in a bit farther and peeked around the corner, searching the floor when Roman blocked my view.

"Looking for something, Jessie?"

I always found him a bit hard to read, but most of the time I felt I could trust him. Today he had a demeanor about him that I couldn't put my finger on.

"Thank god. Did you happen to see a pencil case in here?" I asked hopefully.

"Kind of a strange place for a pencil case," he mused. Sensing my impatience, he quickly responded, "Nope. Sorry, nothing like that here." He cast a glance over his shoulder to prove his point.

I narrowed my eyes suspiciously at him. I had a funny feeling that he wasn't telling the truth.

He pushed past me quickly. "I have to go or I'll be late for class. Sorry I couldn't be much help." He briskly walked away from me, books in hand, looking at his watch.

I sighed. "Well, it's now or never..." I stepped in further to look, scanning the floor. I growled in frustration again. "Where did it go? How can a pencil case disappear?" I turned around and walked out perplexed.

"Damn it! Now I'm really late for class!" I ran as fast as I could, my pink sneakers squeaking on the glossy floor. I skidded to a stop, grabbing the doorframe to stop myself from falling sideways and burst into the classroom. Everyone stared at me as I walked in.

Mr. Wilson glared at me from underneath his glasses, holding a book in his hand, poised midair. "You're late Jessie. Sit down so that I may continue my lecture." He motioned at my desk, his voice stern.

"I'm sorry. But it wasn't my fault!" I started to reply but he raised his palm like a stop sign

"Uh, uh! Sit down!" he responded more sternly this time, his face becoming more flushed. I sneaked a glance to the back of the class where Patricia and Mitchell sat and spotted them smirking.

Casting my eyes downwards, I felt ashamed for creating a spectacle. I dragged my feet to my desk, pulling out my books, and placing them on the table with a thud. I quickly scrambled through my backpack for a pen. My fingers scraped the bottom while I searched for one, then finally grasped it, and placed it beside my books.

Then I quickly grabbed the FM system, a small box that fit in the palm of my hand, slid the power button to ON, stood up, and proceeded to hand it to Mr. Wilson who was waiting for me, palm already out.

"Finished? Thank you." He sighed deeply, placing the loop over his head so the microphone sat on his chest a few inches from his chin.

I sat back down as he began to speak, his voice fading out of my thoughts, while I busily clipped the boots onto my hearing aids, and turned the volume up a notch.

I slunk deeper into my chair, scowling at today's turn of events, feeling miserable. I concentrated as much as I could, but my thoughts kept wandering, unfocused, wondering what to do about the pencil case. I didn't have much money to pay for a new one or for getting more pens, coloring pencils, erasers, calculator, and so on.

It may not mean much to most people, but it was a pain to ask my parents for extra money to purchase yet more school supplies, yet again. I grimaced at the thought of their angry scowls and their response: "Why can't you take better care of your school supplies? Honestly, is that too much to ask?"

I drummed my fingers on the edge of the desk, trying to come up with a feasible plan. I decided when I got home, I'd go through my drawers and see if I could find some old supplies—and felt marginally better.

Finally, the much-anticipated bell rang and I scrambled to snatch up my books and backpack, rushing forward to gather the microphone from Mr. Wilson. As I reached out to grab it, Patricia slammed into my shoulder muttering, "Sorry," with false sincerity, eyes gleaming with malice.

How can anyone behave like a prick and get away with it? I wondered as I marched out the door.

I quickly rushed toward the gym, not daring to be late, changed briskly, and strolled into the large gymnasium. The rest of the class formed a semicircle around Mrs. Roberts and a new instructor. He wore a crisp white uniform with a faded black belt wrapped around his waist.

Mrs. Roberts spoke up. "Okay class, we have a new instructor with us for this month." She gestured toward him. "This is Sensei Jonas. He will be teaching self-defense for the next few weeks. I expect all of you to listen to him and show him the same respect that you show us at school." She turned toward him, nodded at him and said, "They're all yours Sensei Jonas."

He clapped his hands together. "All right group! Glad to see all of you here today!"

I rolled my eyes at his remark since the classes were mandatory, plus he was a bit too perky for me today.

Walking quickly to the front, he pointed to the area in front of him. "Okay, I want everyone to form several lines, spreading out from the sides. Make sure that there is a lot of space all around you," he said cheerfully but with authority, his voice commanding.

I groaned and shuffled toward the front, close to him. The gym was spacious and unbelievably echoing. Despite his loud, booming voice, his words bounced off the walls making them hard to understand. I had no choice but to join the line at the front of the class. He smiled when he spotted me moving in his direction. "Excellent!" he said, clapping his hands eagerly.

As I waited for the rest of the class to line up, I watched him organize the group with ease. He looked strong, even though his uniform hid most of his physique, and walked with a straight back, full of confidence. His dark, short hair was slightly wavy, his moustache neatly trimmed. I gritted my teeth, biting back a tart remark that I couldn't stand moustaches. They covered too much of a person's lips, making it nearly impossible to speech read them. I just hoped that I could follow him during his classes.

Still seething over the callous prank that Patricia and Mitchell pulled on me earlier, I sighed deeply, trying to calm down, and thought, *Could this day get any worse?*

A strong commanding voice broke my train of thought
and I glanced toward Sensei Jonas. "Good job forming the
lines everyone!" He seemed genuinely pleased at the
group's efficiency at lineup which was a simple task for us.

"Now, in Martial Arts, we always begin our classes
with a bow." He strolled back and forth across the front of
the class which was driving me nuts since I was struggling
to hear him and follow his lips while he moved around. I
thought, *Please stand still!* As if on cue, he stopped and
turned to face the class.

"Therefore, I want everyone to put their feet together,
hands on the sides of your legs." As he demonstrated the
pose, he continued. "Now, you are going to bend at the
waist and bow down slowly, okay? "Let's try it now," he
said as he watched us. "Bow toward me."

It felt so strange and foreign to me and I felt deeply
self-conscious of doing it.

"Good job!" he said as we stood upright again. "This
time, I will give a command to let you know when it's time
to bow. As soon as I say Keske, you will promptly bring
your feet together, hands to your sides.

"Let's try it now." He uttered the command quickly
and loudly, "Keske!" and brought his feet sharply together,
slapping his legs with his palms.

"Next, I will call out Rei which means you are to
bow." He looked at us, scanning around the room.
"Ready?" Again, he loudly proclaimed, "Rei!" and bowed at
the waist.

"Very good!" he said as he straightened up and stood at ease. "And you can all relax for a moment."

I listened intently as he talked to us.

"Next we will learn how to do a very simple kick." He spoke with ease, obviously used to speaking in front of many students.

"This type of kick is an excellent way of disarming your opponent, catching them by surprise." He went on to explain in detail, "You see on most people, it hurts to be kicked in the groin, even for the ladies." He saw the looks of surprise on our faces. "Obviously it has the most impact on the men...unless they happen to be wearing a jock," he added as a joke.

"If someone ever tries to grab you, this technique will give you enough time to get away and even deliver another blow if necessary.

"All right, now, what I want everyone to do is place their feet about shoulder width apart, bending your knees slightly." He watched us try out this position as he strolled across the floor.

He walked back to his usual spot. "Now I want you to raise your hands at shoulder height to protect your face. Keep your hands open though. We don't want your opponent to be aware of what you are about to do. A closed fist is a visual sign, an obvious indication that you want to fight. An open hand is simply a defensive gesture."

I raised my hands upward, feeling a bit silly and out of place as he continued with his demonstration.

"Good. Now bring your right knee upward. Hold it there for a second, bring out your leg and point your toes downwards." He raised his leg in unison with us, showing us the movements.

"Okay, and bring it back slowly and place your foot back down.

"Let's do the same thing with the other foot, bring up your knee, extend your leg, and bring it back down," he said, swiftly bringing his own leg down as he spoke.

"Excellent work everyone! And relax. I will demonstrate how it should look at high speed." He stood in front, looking strong and formidable as he concentrated, sending out waves of power. Suddenly he kicked with such force that his uniform snapped sharply and loudly. It was impressive and yet also threatening.

"This time I will do it in combination with a Kiai. Ready? Just watch." He swiftly snapped out his leg and uttered a loud yell that reverberated throughout the gym, startling us. Some of the students staggered backward in surprise. My heart thudded in fear and shock from the sudden burst of energy.

We all looked at each other, eyes wide, murmuring under our breath. "Wow!" "Did you see that?

Now do you see its effectiveness?" He nodded at us, referring to our surprised reactions. "The Kiai comes from our solar plexus. It's a short burst of energy that helps prepare our body for a fight."

He looked at us and pointed a finger upward, adding an afterthought. "Plus it scares the crap out of your opponent." He grinned. "It's a great tool to startle them momentarily.

"Fabulous. Now let's practice these kicks again. This time, do it with a little bit of force. You are all welcome to add a Kiai if you wish to do so."

No one said anything as we were all a bit too shy and self-conscious.

I focused my attention on the kick, feeling a sense of exhilaration as I did. I loved the motion and its power. The more I practiced and the more strength I put behind it, the more I could feel the anger being released. It was as if I was channeling my frustration out through my legs. I could feel the tension flow off my shoulders for the first time all day.

We continued working on our kicks until it was time to dismiss the class. We bowed in response to his command and left the gym toward the changing room. Everyone was abuzz with excitement creating a hum of noise as we quickly changed out of our gym clothes.

CHAPTER 2

Revelation

I woke up, smiling as I glanced out the window. It was starting out to be a beautiful day. The sun was shining brightly, the leaves on the trees exploding in brilliant colors. Parker was curled up beside me, sleeping blissfully. I gently stroked his soft fur. He stirred, blinking his green eyes up at me.

He was named after Peter Parker of Spiderman fame. He'd earned it after I caught him effortlessly climbing the screened in porch and opening the door by pushing the latch with his back paws. I don't know how many times he had escaped using that particular strategy before I saw him in action and began locking the door.

"Sorry, munchkin, didn't mean to wake you." Even without my hearing aids on, I could tell he responded to me by the squeeze of his broad chest and the way his jaws parted briefly as he meowed. I could feel the deep rumbles coming from beneath my fingers. He was happy and purring nonstop.

"I wish I could hang out with you. But I gotta go to school." I got up, stretching as I strolled across the floor toward my closet. There wasn't much of a selection to choose from. I had a handful of hoodies, shirts, and sweaters that hung on the rack. I picked up my clover green hoodie and a pair of well-worn jeans with a large hole in the knee. I loved those jeans. They were comfortable despite being torn in a couple of places where the fabric stretched thinly.

I looked in the mirror, placed some scrunching gel in my hands, and ran it through my hair trying to get some bounce back into my blond curls. I grabbed pink lip gloss from the counter and smoothed it onto my lips, enjoying its glimmer and sweet, fruity taste. There was not much makeup to choose from. Most of it was almost gone and I couldn't afford to buy anymore at the moment. Looking through the meager pile in front of me, I swiped some blush onto my cheeks. I felt grateful that my skin was smooth today. Most of the time it was covered in blemishes that I would try in vain to hide. Plus, I was running dangerously low on concealer.

I put on a pair of simple hoop earrings, pushed the earmolds in, and tucked my hearing aids behind my ears. I checked to make sure they were fitting snuggly to avoid any feedback. I checked my image in the mirror again, liking the transparent green shells of the hearing aids, noticing that they matched my hoodie.

I rummaged through the bottom of my closet, searching for my pink Converse sneakers and backpack. As I placed the backpack on the seat of the chair beside my bed, I grabbed a stack of textbooks from the table and promptly shoved them into the backpack, zipping it closed.

Walking briskly toward the door, I scratched Parker on the head. "Bye Handsome, I'll see you later," I said and released my chocolate-brown corduroy jacket from the hook on the back of the door. It used to belong to my father but he rarely wore it and when I asked him if I could wear it to school, surprisingly he'd agreed.

My feet thumped loudly down the wooden stairs. I grabbed the post at the bottom and swiveled around toward the kitchen table. I picked up an apple from the fruit basket sitting in the center of the wooden table. Mom had several trays of food, mostly puff pastries, ready to be delivered to a client of hers. She did a lot of catering for local businesses as well as weddings and elegant parties. It kept her busy and the house always smelled like a bakery, full of mouthwatering scents. I loved it when she made desserts. It filled the house with a delectable aroma making it feel cozy. Plus she always managed to sneak a few treats off to the side for me to sample. I occasionally would bring a few pieces to school for lunch.

Today she had a couple of small muffins for me, with cream cheese frosting on top.

There was a post-it note beside them, it read:

Jessie, you can have these two muffins for school. Enjoy! Love Mom.

Yes! These were one of my favorite muffins. They were very much like a carrot cake and absolutely addicting. I opened the refrigerator door, pulled out my lunch bag, already packed from the night before and quickly placed a muffin in it. I munched on the other one as I went out the door.

I walked past Mom, with her curly auburn locks touching her shoulder. She wore black slacks and a lovely creamy white blazer. The back doors of the van were open and she was cautiously placing the trays inside it.

"Bye Mom! Thanks for the muffins!" I said, through a mouthful of crumbly muffin, and waved at her as I walked down the gravel lane.

"Glad you like them! Have fun at school honey!" she replied as she glanced past the open doors, smiling.

I cheerfully continued munching on the now dwindling muffin, kicking aside the brightly lit leaves on the ground. The air was crisp and the sun felt comfortably warm on my face. Fall was always my favorite time of the year. I loved it so much that I promised myself that if I ever got married, it would be in the fall, surrounded by its immense beauty and rich palette of colors. The ground thick with snow nearly up to my waist, I thought as I came to a stop in front of the red mailbox, with the name, "McIntyre," on it in faint letters.

Today felt especially more cheerful than usual. There was a buzz of excitement in the air. Partly because it was Friday and partly because tomorrow was my birthday.

I had invited several of the girls from school who seemed nice enough. I didn't know them too well since I didn't particularly belong in their clique. I was more of an acquaintance. I found it intriguing that there were so many different groups of people at school. The choices seemed staggering to me.

Even though it wasn't necessarily a large school, it was a big adjustment for me, coming from a very small rural elementary school. I'd had to change schools since it ended at grade five, it was that small. This one included both middle school and high school, housing approximately three hundred students.

The sound of squeaking brakes broke through my thoughts. Funny, I didn't have to wait long for the bus. I must have been deep in my thoughts to not really notice its arrival. I walked up the worn steps, gripping the handlebars, and promptly sat down on one of the empty seats near the front so I could scramble out as quickly as possible. I couldn't stand being on this bus. Even though it was a relatively short ride of thirty minutes, it seemed like an eternity for me. The kids on the bus were not exactly civilized. They had a tendency to pull ridiculously inane pranks or throw wads of paper at my head to irritate me. They could be at times, unbelievably immature and rude. Honestly, there were days when I wanted to smack the silly grins off their faces.

I did my best to ignore their asinine calls and blonde-haired jokes and simply watched the landscape blur outside the window. After what seemed like an hour of driving past the rolling hills dotted with cows, we edged closer to town. It was surrounded by small subdivisions starting to grow, their cancerous fingers spreading slowly through the countryside.

Beaverdale Middle School/High School loomed on the horizon, surrounded by tall pine trees, their thick branches offering privacy all around the property. Within their green walls, lush grass covered virtually every surface like a thick carpet. It could easily pass for a golf course and country club. The school was fairly simple in design with its red bricks and two story layout. It reminded me of an old library with its tall columns on either side of the doors and a huge clock sitting above the archway.

The bus rolled slowly down the driveway, thankfully coming to a stop. My backpack was already in my hand and I dashed out the door as quickly as I could, feeling a sense of relief to be out of the cramped bus. My thoughts started to wander again as I stepped on the concrete sidewalk leading toward the entrance.

As I marched down the worn-out linoleum, its surface gleaming from a fresh polish, I could spot the distinctive cliques gathered like flocks of geese in the hallways. Or perhaps the phrase, pack of wolves was a more apt description for the group huddled against the lockers as I nudged past them. Their eyes locked on me as they whispered to each other scornfully.

I'm always astounded at the sheer number of groups that form at school. There were simply so many of them, attracting others like a powerful magnet. I really didn't want to get sucked into the wrong group since some of their antics made me rather uncomfortable with them. I was acutely aware of how they would talk behind my back, pointing fingers at me, particularly toward my hearing aids.

I walked past a group of intellectuals, flipping through their notebooks comparing notes. They were a nice bunch of kids, who were mostly polite to me. Although I wouldn't go as far as to describe them as geeks, they were simply smart enough to stay out of trouble and get impressive grades. They were an ambitious bunch, all striving to get scholarships and be noticed by the top universities. I nodded at them cheerfully, "Hi, guys!" and they waved back at me, returning my salutation.

Another distinctive group gathered around the lockers on my left. They were all sharply dressed and well groomed, looking like models straight out of a fashion magazine. They reeked of wealth, clearly not afraid to show it off, and were obviously spoiled. Their views toward me seemed neutral. They rarely gave me a hard time when we crossed paths. However, I could tell by the looks they gave me, they didn't exactly approve of me, tilting their noses up at me. I looked down, feeling out of their league in my casual clothes. I practically looked like a homeless person standing next to them.

I turned right, down another corridor passing the gymnasium. I spotted several familiar faces belonging to my teammates in intramural basketball. They were chatting animatedly with the other jocks, a couple of them who were all-star athletes and immensely popular throughout the school.

I slowed down as I approached them. The guys looked over their shoulders and started to walk away. *Weird,* I thought. *Didn't they want to say hello?* They strode toward the changing rooms, bouncing the basketball on the floor without looking at me. We had exchanged polite conversation in the past, mostly about sports whenever we crossed paths. Today, they seemed cold toward me.

I dismissed their lack of interest with a shrug of my shoulders and shouted a greeting to the rest of the group.

Their names were Donna, Amber, Jackie, Kathy, and believe it or not, Buffy. I wondered what kind of parent would name their child Buffy. All I could visualize were fluffy bunnies every time I that name. At first, I thought it was her nickname. Nope, it truly was her legal name.

Last week I had invited them to my birthday, which was tomorrow and I was checking with them to make sure that they were indeed coming. As I came to a stop in front of them, they were already picking up their books and backpacks, getting ready to go to class.

"Wait! Before you go, I...um, just wanted to confirm that all of you are coming over to my place tomorrow."

They exchanged knowing glances at each other and murmured, "Yes," or "Not a problem." They smiled at me, slightly too wide to be genuinely convincing.

Odd. I thought. *What is going on today? Everyone is acting so strange.*

They started walking away. "Great!" I called after them. "I'll see you tomorrow!" They waved at me as they left, heads together in deep conversation.

I stopped by the small office to pick up the listening device that was sitting in the charging station, checked briefly that it was fully charged before continuing on to my first class.

The morning classes went by quickly. I barely noticed them because I was so absorbed in my thoughts about the party, planning what to do. I was thrilled at the opportunity to invite this particular group, they seemed like a good bunch of players and quite talented in sports.

I wouldn't go as far as to describe myself as good as them but I was certainly athletic and enjoyed it. Playing sports wasn't always easy for me. In the gym the sounds echoed badly, the squeaking shoes multiplied in volume, making it hard to hear the referee's whistles. I can't even begin to count how many times I kept on playing long after the whistle had been blown while everyone stared at me in exasperation.

I tried hard to keep up with my teammates and pay attention to the game but there were times when I missed a critical play, which caused them to doubt my playing ability.

My coach tried to be supportive of me, particularly in regards to my hearing loss and its shortcomings, but there were times when I could tell she was reaching the breaking point in her patience with me.

It had become apparent that some of my other teammates couldn't stand being near me and would deliberately sit at the far end of the bench, away from me. They didn't make any effort to hide their disgust toward me and they often acted if I was contagious.

Not this group though. They played alongside me and treated me like one of their own. Which is why I chose them to spend the day with me this weekend.

At lunch, I sat down in an empty slot at a crowded table. There was space on either side of me, which was fine.

The auditorium was packed as usual, loud with the buzzing noise of hundreds of voices talking all at once. I looked across the table as I ate, puzzled by the glances toward me. I looked over my shoulder to see if anyone was behind me. Nope, there was no one there and no reason that I knew of for the odd expressions on their faces. *What is going on?* I wondered, suddenly feeling really insecure.

I was relieved when afternoon classes were over. I plunked down the FM system in its slot, grateful that I didn't have to wear it for the rest of the day. I always felt conspicuous whenever I used it for class and felt particularly as if all of the eyes were on me as I handed over the microphone to the teachers in front of the class. It was embarrassing at times to have to show them how to turn it on or off. They conveyed their displeasure that I had to become the teacher and they became the student even for a few moments.

I was thankful to be home after a long day. Throwing my books on the bed and hooking the backpack on my chair. I headed downstairs and made myself a cup of tea while I reheated a plate of casserole in the microwave for supper.

Mom had left another note on the counter stating the she would be late coming home tonight. There was a stack of DVDs beside it on the table. Apparently, she'd brought home rentals of the latest releases for tomorrow's party.

The microwave dinged, indicating my dinner was ready to eat. I proceeded to carry it over to the kitchen table with a handful of utensils. As I sat down, my eye caught the brightly colored glossy magazine sitting on the chair. It was one of those fashion magazines that Mom loved to read, and she had been flipping through the current issue.

I idly flipped through the pages as I ate, admiring the elegant clothes the models wore. I loved the cheerful colors and styles, wishing I could afford a wardrobe like that. I had always wondered what it would be like to feel so sophisticated and glamorous. I ran my fingers over the full-page ad of a lovely cable knit sweater, imagining the softness of it.

I looked through the rest of the magazine, stopping to read the entertainment section, getting caught up in the lifestyles of the stars. I knew in the back of my mind that I had to take it with a grain of salt, that most of it was designed to create a buying frenzy amongst consumers to generate ridiculous amounts of money. Still, it helped to be up to date so I could at least follow the conversations my classmates had during breaks.

I groaned as I got up, feeling some stiffness in my neck from reading. I stretched out the kinks building between my shoulder blades. Gathering up the plate, I put it into the dishwasher, picked up Parker's bowl, and refilled it with fresh kibble. He promptly appeared by my side meowing as soon as I put it down. As I petted him, I could feel him purring with delight beneath my fingers. I laughed at the thought of him somehow knowing when there was food nearby. *It's like he has a sixth sense.*

I peered out the window over the sink, noticing the sky was already a deep cobalt blue. *Hmm, it's going to be winter soon. It's getting dark much earlier now.*

"Well, at least it's going to be a beautiful day tomorrow, perfect fall weather." I remarked to Parker, who was currently my only audience. He glanced up at me, between mouthfuls of kibble, blinked, sending a cheerful "chirrup" my way in response.

I loved the way he talked to me, mostly perky meows and throaty chirps that were halfway between a purr and meow. I found it oddly endearing that I could still understand him without my hearing aids. I bent down and scratched the top of his furry head before dashing up the stairs to my room.

My dad's old iBook sat on my desk waiting to be used. He had given it to me last year so that I could do my homework and browse on the internet without bugging him to use it. I had been stunned that he gave it to me, even though it wasn't exactly new, but nonetheless I was thrilled to have my own computer. The only stipulation was that I had to keep it at home for fear of it being stolen at school. And the way my track record was at the moment with so many things disappearing, he was right.

I browsed through the internet, painfully slowly I might add, since we were still on dial-up. Our town had promised, for five years in a row, that all streets in the rural area would be equipped with high-speed access any day now. I snorted at that statement since the council was notorious for changing their minds at the last minute, choosing not to provide the services we could use around here.

After a while, I became bored and noticed the time. It was getting late and I wanted to be bright-eyed for tomorrow. I was excited about it, looking forward to spending time with my teammates.

Parker jumped up on the bed with me, curling up near my feet purring away happily. "Night, munchkin," I said to him before turning out the light.

I awoke to a bright room, the sun filling up every wall and corner with its light. I immediately felt cheerful and nearly skipped out of my room, giddy in my PJs. I pranced down the stairs to the kitchen and saw a note on the counter from Mom.

Happy Birthday Jessie! I'll be at a wedding all day and your dad is at the Library doing research. There is pizza in the freezer and the cupcakes are for your party. Have a great time! Love Mom.

Beside the note was a glorious display of cupcakes, stacked on a three-tiered rack, all lavishly spread with ruby, lavender and pink icing complete with delicate flowers on the top. I gasped in delight, admiring the spectrum of colors. "She must've made these last night after I went to bed," I whispered to myself.

After I gave Parker his breakfast and scarfed down mine, I quickly vacuumed the floor, tidied up the living room, put the DVDs on the small table in front of the TV, gathered a few CDs, and placed them on the table as well. It wasn't much of a choice since I really didn't listen to a lot of music, but it was better than nothing. I selected the most current magazines from around the house and set them on the table for good measure, hoping that it would be a great conversation starter.

I did a mental checklist, looked around the house making sure everything was presentable and ready to go. Satisfied, I went upstairs, got dressed and put on whatever makeup I had left. I didn't really know what to wear and chose to keep it casual with a pink zippered hoodie, long sleeved pastel green waffle shirt, and jeans.

I pulled my hair up into a simple ponytail, letting the blond curls cascade around my head like a halo. Glancing in the mirror, I swiped the pink gloss on my lips and went downstairs to set up the kitchen table.

Once I was certain there were enough plates and utensils, I plunked them down in front of each chair. The pink napkins were carefully folded and tucked beside each plate. Next, I added glasses and a pitcher of pink lemonade in the center. Hmm, it needs something else...I snapped my fingers. "I know what will work!" And I dashed outside with a knife. The entire field behind our house was filled with tall golden sunflowers, gently swaying in the breeze. Walking down the well-worn path between the sunflowers, I cut down a few stalks, inhaling their sweet scent as I went back into the kitchen and placed them in a vase.

I glanced at the clock in the kitchen, realizing that it was getting close to the time for the guests' arrival. I quickly grabbed two clear bowls along with a package of M&M's and some chips. I poured them into their respective bowls and placed them near the TV.

What was I forgetting? I had the impression I was missing something. I thumped the heel of my hand into my forehead realizing that I needed to preheat the oven for the pizza. Scampering over to the oven, I quickly turned it on, pulled the pizza from the freezer, and plunked it down on the cookie tray.

"Now everything is ready. Perfect!" I clasped my hands together, hoping that it would all go smoothly. It was nearly one o'clock, just in time. I walked over to the kitchen, looking down the driveway. "Nope. Nothing yet." I sighed nervously, rubbing my palms together.

Not being able to stand the tension any longer, I went outside on to the porch and sat in the swing to wait. It really was a remarkable day as a cool breeze gently brushed my hair, the sun warmed my face. As I waited, I admired the dazzling colors blooming across the landscape. The trees were stunning in the strong sunlight, seemingly determined to celebrate the season in a blaze of glory.

The squirrels ran around the lawn, digging under the leaves and searching for the acorns strewn all over the place. Goldfinches were everywhere, supposedly stocking up on their food, frantically gathering as much energy as possible for the winter. A chipmunk suddenly appeared in front of me, sitting on the porch railing, looking equally as stunned as I. He sat rooted to that spot for a minute until he started to scratch his ear and chittered loudly adding to the cacophony of chirps all around me.

Strange, it felt like quite a bit of time had passed, perhaps twenty minutes and yet there was no sign of anyone. Curious, I went back into the house to check the time and was surprised to discover that thirty minutes had already gone by.

A shock of cold fear ran through me and I briefly wondered if I had made a mistake on the invitations. I thought about it and was sure that I put down the correct time on them. Pacing back and forth, checking the clock every few minutes, I kept my eyes on the driveway through the window.

After an hour had passed, I somberly realized that no one was going to appear in the driveway. *Well, not for me anyway.* Feeling utterly dejected, I stood there dumbstruck as it truly dawned on me that I wasn't going to have a party after all. A range of emotions raced through me from anger to shock to shame and finally deep sorrow. It felt like a tight band had suddenly been constricted across my chest and I couldn't breathe. My hands started to shake. I held them tightly to my chest.

Deep sobs racked my body and tears streamed freely down my cheeks. I sank down on the floor beside the couch near the TV and cried uncontrollably. I tried to watch a DVD but the tears blurred my vision so much that I couldn't even see the screen. I folded my knees up, wrapping my arms around my legs, gripping them as hard as I could.

Never in my life had I felt so rejected and worthless. My heart ached so badly that I literally thought it would break in two. I sat on the floor until I was stiff and sore and the tears had run out. By now, I was furious. Angry at myself for being such a fool, believing that I deserved to have friends like that and be able to trust them.

I stood up, stormed across the room and started putting everything back in the cupboards. I threw the pizza back into the freezer forcefully, cranking the oven off so hard that the knob nearly snapped.

I snatched up the magazines and threw them into the recycling box. Angrily I emptied the bowls of M&M's and chips into the trash. Grabbing the pitcher, I poured its contents into the sink, too angry to put it away properly. On my way out of the kitchen, I picked up a cupcake from the display rack and stomped up the stairs.

Once I reached my room, I slammed the door shut, startling Parker awake from peaceful slumber on my bed. I sent a terse apology his way and promptly sat down in front of my laptop. I waited impatiently for it to establish a connection, muttering to myself, "Frigging dial up!" getting more impatient by the minute.

As soon as it was online, I immediately sent an email to all of my "so called friends" asking them where they were. Three of them replied within minutes, claiming that they were out of town or had a family emergency. I narrowed my eyes suspiciously as I read their lame excuses and felt another wave of tears emerging. I felt rejected again, and my chest tightened painfully as I closed the laptop. As the tears dripped onto my cheeks, I crawled into my bed, sobbing, curling up into a tight ball.

I had fallen asleep and woke up with a start. I looked at the alarm clock by my bed and its bright LED lights declared that it was just a few minutes past three in the afternoon. The tightness in my chest did not dissipate even as I stretched and stood up to gaze out the window. My body felt heavy and drained as I shuffled my feet across the bare wooden floor. I stared at the uneaten cupcake on the desk, long forgotten and looking so forlorn. I reached out and took a bite without tasting it. I felt so numb, still in shock from what happened earlier and tired from crying.

Mumbling as I went out the door, I called Parker and asked if he wanted to go out for a walk with me. I was hoping that the fresh air would help clear my head and I honestly didn't feel like staying inside where it seemed so claustrophobic and dark.

Parker often enjoyed our strolls, staying by my side, stopping to sniff the leaves or pounce on a mole tunneling beneath his feet. I loved watching him leap high into the air while chasing a butterfly, dancing across the grass to capture it. He was so powerful and yet there was a sense of grace in his stance.

I knew it was silly but having him with me outside made me feel safer. He was very alert to our surroundings and would often freeze at strange noises, reacting to sounds that were beyond my range of hearing.

I had seen him chase animals off our property including a large red fox, its tail bigger than him. He came back without a scratch on him, satisfied that he had done his job protecting me. He had always been fiercely protective of me and in many ways behaved more like a guard dog or in my case a hearing-ear cat.

We strolled through the back door, down the steps toward the woods at the end of the field. Our backyard consisted of sunflowers as far as the eye could see. We had two fields that surrounded our property, separated by a worn path from our house to the woods. Their tall stalks swayed in the breeze as if dancing to music hidden in the wind. Chickadees occasionally swooped down to pluck a seed from their large golden heads.

I kicked at the leaves with my feet, sending them flying through the air. Suddenly Parker pranced upward and snagged a leaf with his front paws midair. Impressed, I giggled at his playfulness and continued to kick the leaves along the pathway, tucking my hands into my sweatshirt pockets. Every so often, he would wiggle his rump, watching me then dash off to capture a leaf.

Once in a while, a grasshopper would leap high in the air in front of us and Parker would seemingly float upward after them, like a majestic ballet dancer doing acrobatic spins and twirls. I laughed, enjoying his dance in the field, feeling my heart becoming just a little bit lighter.

As we stopped at the edge of the woods, the worn path was directly in front of us, gently curving downwards into the valley. The sun cast long shadows across the colorful floor, appearing more like a quilt as the leaves blanketed the ground in a myriad of ruby and deep amber.

We walked noisily down the path, the leaves crunching beneath our feet, mine sounding much louder, of course. I looked down at him as we continued our stroll and at that precise moment, without any prompting, he gazed up at me blinking, and I swore that I saw him smile.

The path curved to the left near a large tree, its thick roots protruding at the base of its trunk. I sat down between them, feeling the rough bark cradle me like a comfortable chair, and drew my knees to my chest. Parker also sat down beside me, his back paws peeking out from beneath his furry tummy, front paws perfectly aligned in front, poised like an Egyptian Sphinx.

I looked up, leaning my head against the bark, feeling so very small in such a large forest. Even though the trees were dense around here, it was bright and airy as the sunlight filtered through the golden foliage. Sitting down there at the bottom of the valley created a sense of enormous trees sprouting from all around me, straining to reach blue sky, gradually becoming thinner toward the top.

Despite Parker's presence, I suddenly felt so alone and incredibly insignificant. A fresh wave of tears streamed down my face without warning, my chest becoming unbearably tight. The pain made it hard to breathe.

I tried, I really tried to make new friends at school but they seemed to shun me. They never gave me a chance to connect with them. It was difficult enough having to change schools again, surrounded by a sea of unfamiliar faces.

As if sensing my sorrow, Parker reached up with his paw and touched my cheek. I looked down at him and said thank you as I gently touched the soft fur between his ears.

Feeling miserable, I closed my eyes, letting the sun dry my tears, feeling its warmth on my skin. I took several deep breaths, inhaling the crisp fresh air and musty leaves. A breeze fluttered across my face and I opened my eyes upward at the blue sky, watching the trees sway above me like a moving ceiling. The leaves shook like thousands of hands clapping.

Interesting. I watched the trees continue to clap as if they were giving a standing ovation to an impressive concert, a symphony of colors celebrating the season.

As if on cue for an encore, a solemn leaf spiraled downwards, swirling around the trunk of the tree, circling crazily toward me. I gasped, stunned at this marvelous trick. *How is that possible?* I watched it flutter down, landing at Parker's feet. He reached out and tapped it with his paw, equally as curious.

I stared at in awe, feeling incredibly lucky to have witnessed such a stunning feat. Wow, that was unusual, since it meant that for once I had to be in the right spot at the right time to have seen that, as I stroked Parker's, fur warmed by the sun.

I stayed for a while longer, watching the leaves shake and shimmer in the wind, as the shadows stretched out in front of us, their long fingers boldly painting the forest floor in shades of blue. I felt the sun drift further away, hidden behind thick trees. Feeling cooler now, I decided to go back.

"Okay buddy, time to go." I looked down and gave him a hug, enjoying his warm fur against my skin. I picked him up and carried him in my arms as I walked back up the hill. The sky was filled with golden puffy clouds and lavender streaks as the sun slowly set behind the horizon.

As we arrived on the porch, I spotted Mom's van and quickly became concerned. *How was I going tell her that no one showed up?*

I put my hand on the doorknob, fearing her reaction. When I stepped into the kitchen, she was cleaning the counter and putting the empty trays in the sink. I tried to sneak past her but at that moment, Parker leapt out of my arms, landing on the floor with a thud, prompting her to turn around.

"Jessie! I wondered where you were," she said as she dried her hands with a towel. "Didn't your friends want any cupcakes?" She pointed toward the untouched display.

I stammered, feeling embarrassed, my face burning. "Um, no one came." I stared at the floor, not wanting to see her reaction.

"What?" she exclaimed loudly. I glanced upward at her as tears welled up behind my eyes. "Oh, I'm sorry honey." Walking toward me with open arms, she pulled me into a hug. She rocked me back and forth as if trying to calm a colicky baby.

As she released me from her embrace, she gave me a kiss on the forehead, determined to brighten what was left of my birthday. "Well, you know what? Who needs friends like them? You deserve better than that. You are far too special for people like them to really appreciate the kind of person you are. If they are not willing to make an effort to get to know you, then they're not worth it."

I sighed, having heard that little quip before when I was younger. She strolled over to the couch, picked up an elegantly wrapped pink box covered with chocolate brown polka dots with lavish bow on top.

"I wanted to wait until I was home to give this to you," she said as she passed it to me.

Still feeling insecure, afraid that I might cry again, I kept my eyes on the gift in front of me as I lifted the pink tissue paper, happy to have received a gift. I nearly squealed with delight once I saw what was hidden in the pink folds.

"Oh, I love it Mom!" I lifted it out of the box, admiring the shimmering effect in the light. It was a pair of soft Dorm pants in a rich cobalt blue with golden stars, crescent moons, and elegant birds in flight. Along with it was a long-sleeved waffle shirt also in cobalt blue, perfect for casual wear or as PJs. I couldn't wait to wear them tonight. They looked so cozy and simply fun. To me, clothes were a real treat since a lot of the items in my closet were second hand, mostly given to me by our relatives. It was a treasure to receive a brand new outfit.

Included in the box was a card, I picked it up, opened it, and grabbed a pair of shiny earrings as they slipped out. The handwritten note in the card read, *To reach the stars, all you have to do is believe. Love Mom.*

The silver earrings were shaped like stars as they cascaded down the miniature chain link. They were stunning and I looked forward to wearing them at school.

For the first time all day, I felt a sense of hope that maybe tomorrow would be a better day.

"Aww, these are great Mom. Thank you!" I said as I gathered up the gifts.

"Glad you like them. I knew that you would like the Bluebirds on the pants."

I smiled as I admired them. "I love them. They are a sign of good luck, especially if you see them. "I'm sorry about the cupcakes," I uttered as I turned toward the stairs.

"Don't worry about it. At least, there's more for us to enjoy." She smiled, trying to be supportive. "Did you want any supper?" she asked, her brows creasing in concern.

"No, it's okay, I'm not really hungry." I carried the gifts in my arms as I went upstairs to my room, relieved that I didn't cry, yet.

I pulled on the PJs, admiring the deep blue background and iridescent gold shapes on the surface. After I brushed my teeth and scrubbed my face clean, I crawled into bed, pulling the blanket up to my chin, waiting for the pain of hurt and shame to go away. My eyes grew heavy and unfocused as I relaxed, falling into a deep slumber.

Golden shapes shimmered in front of me, floating upward past Parker. I looked down and saw where they were coming from, my pants seemed to blur as the stars lifted up and swirled delicately around me. For a moment there, I felt confused wondering what happened to my blanket and decided to shrug it off, more interested in what was happening now.

The stars sparkled and glowed, surrounding me with a feeling of intense warmth and love. It was an incredible feeling of joy, filling my heart with happiness. It was like being surrounded by a sea of golden, glittering facets of light. I could feel my chest glow with warmth as I watched it shimmer and twinkle all around me. I tried to reach out and touch it, my fingers grasped at nothing, seemingly going right through it. It was as if a blanket full of pure love enveloped me. My heart seemed to grow bigger, filling up with bliss.

It started to dissipate and a shimmering golden figure appeared in front of me. His features were strong and chiseled, resembling a handsome statue of Apollo, holding a sword with a shield strapped across his shoulders. He spoke to me but his voice did not come out of his mouth, rather I heard it in my head, deep and bassy.

"Who are you?" I asked, curiously staring at the figure in front of me. It was strange since I felt no fear of him and had this sense that we had met before. There was an underlying feeling of something familiar about him.

He turned his head to the side, clearly amused. "You already know who I am." He glanced at Parker who was still sound asleep by my feet.

"What?" I looked at him, back at Parker, then at him again, trying to make sense of his cryptic remark. "Nooo...It can't be." I looked at him, puzzled. "Parker?"

"Yes," he responded, appearing genuinely pleased. "In essence, I am your guide and protector. This is my spirit form."

"Wow. You're beautiful," I remarked as I stared at him.

His body seemed to be made of tiny golden granules that sparkled whenever he moved. He blinked his eyes and at that moment, I saw the resemblance to Parker. His eyes were what looked familiar.

"I have chosen this form so I may speak directly with you. I'm here to remind you to not lose your sense of Hope. Your mother was correct in her message to you. Whenever you need inspiration, all you have to do is look for the Northern Star. It will guide you in the right direction." He spoke softly, his voice soothing.

His features were becoming softer, the twinkling lights becoming brighter. His voice was starting to fade. "Don't forget, I will always be with you. We are all connected."

As the shimmer faded, his faced dissolved into a golden translucent cloud of sparkling dust. It swirled lazily around Parker and disappeared into his fur. He raised his head and blinked his eyes, revealing a golden glow. His fur seemed to shimmer for a moment.

CHAPTER 3

Foggy Day

I thought I was getting over the pain and betrayal of my birthday, that everything was finally turning for the better. I was slowly finding the courage and strength I needed to rebuild myself, to feel whole again. Until one day I got the distinct feeling that something was wrong. I couldn't put my finger on it and wondered if I was just being paranoid.

A few days later, I woke up with a start, drenched in sweat, gasping and frantically pawing the air. The last bit of the nightmare I'd had was fading into a dark fog in my memory. I was panting rapidly, scared out of my wits, except that I couldn't remember why. I searched deep in my mind, trying desperately to recollect the dream, grasping at the smoky edges of the faint images.

All I could recall was that it felt cold, foreboding. I could sense the danger within it. It was such a bad feeling it left me wondering if it was an omen, perhaps a premonition of what was yet to happen. I shivered at the thought, rubbing my arms, warming up the goose bumps.

I shivered again and headed for the closet, reaching for a warm black sweater and light pink Henley shirt along with my gray jeans. I rifled through the drawers for underwear and thick gray socks, and headed straight to the bathroom to change.

Once I finished putting on my literally barely-there make up, I strode back to my bedroom, tucked my PJs under my pillow, and picked up my hearing aids from the top of the small dresser by the bed. It took a moment for me to adjust to the sounds entering my ears, going from absolute silence to suddenly hearing the hum of the furnace and the loud creak of my feet on the old wooden floorboards.

Looking out the window, I saw a dense gray fog, I could only see about twenty feet. Beyond that the trees disappeared into the soft mist. It reflected my mood, which was equally as foggy and depressing.

I went downstairs with my ever-growing backpack, grabbed an empty bowl, poured cereal and milk into it, and started munching on the crunchy granola, sipping orange juice between bites.

I glanced out the large kitchen windows and could swear the fog had gotten thicker within the last few minutes, closing in on me.

Running out of time, I dashed outside, locking the door behind me, and moved quickly down the lane. I could barely see the red mailbox in the distance. It wasn't until I was within ten feet of it that I finally spotted it.

I wondered if the buses had been cancelled and started to panic, glancing at my watch. I decided to wait for another ten minutes, hoping that it wouldn't show.

After what seemed like an eternity, I was considering turning around to head back home when the yellow bus materialized through the thick mist and my hopes plummeted.

Crap. I guess with the way my luck was going these days, I shouldn't be surprised. I thought darkly, as the bus came to a screeching halt in front of the mailbox.

The ride to school was pure torture and moved at a snail's pace. I dashed out the door as soon as it stopped, glad to be out of the yellow tank. I made my usual rounds, picking up the microphone and receiver, slithering to stop at one of the tables in Mr. Brown's class.

Sitting beside me was Robin, a strikingly good-looking classmate of mine, who was currently sketching furiously into his notebook. He always dressed sharply enough to look as if he stepped out of a GQ ad. Today he wore a light blue shirt with the collar flipped up Elvis style with a black v-shaped varsity sweater over the top and black jeans.

I had always gotten the impression that he was a bit of a high society type of person, based on his politeness and impeccable manners. I remembered hearing a rumor that his father was a politician with deep pockets who was a major influence in the city.

On several occasions, I had tried to engage him in meaningful conversation but they were always brief, filled with just a few mundane words. I kept getting the impression that he was constantly on guard. It was as if someone was keeping a short leash on him, acutely aware that his actions would have an impact on his family, namely his father.

I turned my head sideways to get a better look at what he was sketching. I loved his ideas. He was brilliant in designing creative posters and I always looked forward to viewing his next masterpiece. This one made me laugh. "Moose? Ha! I love it!" I remarked once I got a glimpse of his drawing.

He looked up at me, smiling, pleased and pushed the sketch toward me. I picked it up, admiring his skillful strokes of a simple yet handsome moose, with the word "MOOSE" in capital letters beneath it. It was strikingly similar to the popular franchise, "Roots," clearly a take-off the brand name.

"This is great Robin. I love the tongue in cheek humor here. That's a fantastic moose," I said honestly.

"Thanks," he said. "I'm considering doing a silk screen on shirts with it." His eyes beamed, no doubt from the dollar signs floating in his head. It would definitely boost his popularity another notch.

His blond hair fell over his forehead as he spoke, adding to his already handsome features. He was tall and walked with a confident stride, making him irresistible to just about everybody, reeling them in with his charm.

Not only was he the class Rep, he was also involved with the Yearbook crew, clearly exuding the charisma of a strong leader. He could easily be the next Prime Minister of Canada.

He looked up at me as I thought about that, imagining his future self. "What? You've got this far away look about you," he asked curiously, chin in his hand, tapping the pencil on the table with the other hand.

"Huh? Oh, I was thinking that since you're so talented and organized, you could easily be the next Prime Minister of Canada." I smiled at him as I spoke.

"Ha! Nooo, I wouldn't go that far. Thanks for the vote of confidence though. I'm not quite that smart," he replied earnestly.

I could feel the ice between us thaw. Surprised by his remark, I gushed, "Are you kidding me? You're one of the smartest people I know."

I could swear that he blushed just before he turned his head away, running his fingers through his hair.

Oops, I think I went one step too far. Damn it. I thought, the air suddenly feeling a bit colder, the distance growing between us again.

He turned back, his piercingly blue eyes facing me, suddenly shy. "Do you really think so?"

Before I could respond, Mr. Brown interrupted us as he started the class, telling everyone to have a seat and open their textbooks to page forty-five. Robin and I looked at each other from time to time with shy smiles as Mr. Brown discussed Art History.

At the end of class, I approached Robin. "Maybe I could buy one of your Moose shirts if I scrounged up enough money?"

"Yeah, sure. That would be awesome." He was polite, becoming reserved once more, slipping further away from me. He walked away and disappeared into the noisy hallway.

And there he goes. Like a fish out to the great big sea.

I sighed, disappointed that he couldn't be more than friends with me. I wondered what I was doing wrong and pondered it for the rest of the day. The classes went by like a blur as teachers eagerly doled out more homework like candy, adding yet more heavy textbooks to my overflowing backpack.

I trudged back to the bus, watching the mist float through the air, like maniacal ghosts hovering just above the ground. Its thick swirls made my hair insanely frizzy. I gritted my teeth, feeling self-conscious and trying unsuccessfully to smooth my hair.

It was a miserable ride home, the cold dampness chilling me to the bone. The mood was dull, and oppressive, and lay heavy on my mind.

My boots squelched through the muddy lane as I pulled the hood of my jacket over my head, switching my backpack from one shoulder to another, trying to ease the ache in my neck. I could feel a headache forming and hoped it wasn't going to end up as a migraine.

I dimly realized that something was wrong when I stepped through the door and tried flicking the light switch on. Huh? What happened to the lights? Looking around, I noticed that the house was dark and utterly cold. I shivered as I gratefully plunked down the backpack by the stairs.

I checked the other lights, flicking them on and off, but nothing happened. "Well, that's just craptastic." I personally didn't like dark places and I could feel the darkness closing in on me, trying to smother me. My heart pounded in fear, making me feel like a scared six year old again.

I rifled through the kitchen drawers and found a working flashlight, and went to a storage closet filled with camping equipment, courtesy of my older brother Ken, who was a teaching assistant in Outdoor Recreation at Lakehead University. I rummaged through the musty items until I found what I was looking for and pulled out the battery operated Coleman's Lantern. I clicked it on, watching it glow, feeling a sense of relief that it still worked.

My clothes were damp and cold from walking in the mist, prompting me to go upstairs and change into dry ones. I pulled on my thick shamrock green sweatpants and navy blue hoodie. I sighed deeply, feeling the tension in my neck, frustrated at the bad luck. It irked me that I couldn't sit down to use the TV or my laptop.

Rolling my neck and shoulders as I went back downstairs, I stomped toward the fireplace, searching for a lighter on top of the mantel. Once I found it, I placed the lantern on the coffee table, picked up a couple of logs from beside the fireplace, arranged them in the center, added a few pieces crumbled newspaper plus a couple of pine cones from a nearby basket.

I flicked the lighter underneath the newspaper, hoping it would catch. Of all the things in the world at which I sucked, this was the one that needed to work. After a second or two, the flames feebly flickered then blossomed to life, their fingers dancing merrily along the edges of the wood. "Sweet! It worked!" I scooted backward, watching the flames and hoping it would continue to burn.

Feeling hungry and in the mood for something cheerful for a change, I went into the kitchen, found what I was searching for, piled it onto a plate, and put it on the table by the fire. Looking around on either side of the fireplace, I spotted the hot dog fork and carried them over to the table. Smiling, I sat down in front of the warm fire and placed the hot dog on the tines, and swung it around into the flames.

I watched the flames lick the hot dog as I turned it around slowly, roasting all sides. The warmth of the fire helped ease the cold dampness away from me. Satisfied that it was cooked, I carefully removed the hot dog from the fork and put in on the plate. I plucked a marshmallow from the fluffy pile and gingerly stuck it on the end of the fork and moved it into the flames.

As I munched on the hot dog I watched the marshmallow puff up and brown lightly, remembering the summers that my family had spent on the beach sitting by the campfire.

As soon as it was brown all over, I pulled it out of the fire and placed it on top of the chocolate bar and graham cracker. I smushed down the marshmallow with glee and brought the warm S'more to my lips, savoring the smoky sweetness.

While I nibbled on the goopy S'more, an idea began to form in the back of my mind. Once I finished, I dashed to my backpack, yanked out my sketchbook and pencil crayons, and brought them back to the table. I sat down crossed legged on the floor in front of the fireplace and began sketching, my pencil moving swiftly on the pad of paper.

I started with a large circle, adding an island at the base with two palm trees sprouting from the center. It may have been a bit trite but I liked the simplicity of it, a perfect escape for my mind to someplace well away from the current dreariness.

I colored in the orb with shades of vibrant orange, filled the leaves of the palm trees with a rich green, added a touch of brown and purple for the bark and gentle strokes of soft golden yellow for the island. It certainly was not a stroke of genius or anywhere close to the creativeness as Robin's Moose design, but all I wanted to do was have fun.

I glanced up at the fire noticing that it had died down considerably while I was so focused on my sketching. Closing my sketchbook and putting away the pencil crayons, I gathered the plates and put them on the kitchen counter. I put away the surplus marshmallows and crackers, hanging onto the rest of the chocolate bar for myself. I picked up my backpack and sketchbook along with the Coleman lantern and marched upstairs to my room. It was already getting dark outside, casting even darker shadows in my room.

I dumped everything at the foot of my bed and put the lantern on the table beside the defunct lamp. Grabbing the sketchbook once again, I continued to do some more coloring, enhancing the shading of the scenery.

Pulling back the crinkly wrapper, I took a bit of the chocolate, letting it melt on my tongue. Parker must've heard the wrapper because he came running in to investigate, meowing. His Irish green eyes twinkled with delight and his caramel tail swished back and forth in anticipation.

"And where were you when I was cooking hot dogs downstairs?" I asked him. He turned his head to the side, looking as cute as possible and meowed again. "Sorry, cats can't have chocolate." Sensing defeat, he jumped off the bed and padded away.

Moments later, he jumped back on carrying a small stuffed toy in the shape of bird and put it down in front of me, nosing it toward me. "Oh! That's so sweet! Thank You!

"I still can't give you any of this, though. It'll make you so sick." I reached out, stroking the fur on his chest, feeling the soft rumble of his purring. He stretched out on the bed beside me as I worked on my drawing, not paying attention to the time as my mind wandered aimlessly.

The sun felt so good on my skin. I was looking up at the sky enjoying its warmth and embracing the gentle breeze that swirled around me. It was a refreshing change from the depressing gray skies we'd had lately. My mood had been sour of late clearly reflecting the never-ending rolling clouds.

I was growing tired of wearing long sleeved sweaters and bulky layers just to stay warm against the damp cold. It seeped everywhere, through the walls and through my mind. The gray skies seemed to blanket my soul as well.

I inhaled the fresh scent of the sea as I listened to the seagulls cry out occasionally. I found their odd calls silly at times. They sounded like they were giggling maniacally as if a clown was trying to escape from their throats.

The more I thought about it, the more bizarre the concept became. *How can a seagull possibly giggle?*

I decided that this train of thought was derailing fast and tried to shift my focus elsewhere, concentrating on searching for seashells instead. I sighed, relaxing already as my eyes roamed the glittering surface. My toes gripped the tiny shifting granules as I strolled casually along the beach, squelching slightly in the damp spots.

There were tufts of soft white feather woven in the tall reeds. I bent down to pick one up, my fingers grasping its graceful curve and elegant stem. I traced the edge of the feather with my finger, feeling its softness, marveling at its simple beauty.

I continued my stroll down the long stretch of the sandy beach, casting glances out toward the waves. The tips sparkled merrily, sending thousands of dazzling diamonds into my eyes. I instantly felt rich just looking at it.

Amongst the top of the rolling tips, far out in the distance, almost sitting right on the horizon was a Catamaran with its white and red sails dancing its own tune to the sea's rhythm.

Something poked at my toe and I looked down. As I did, a smile slowly spread across my face. It was a beautiful creamy white seashell with gentle ridges swooping over its back. I picked it up feeling as giddy as if I was on a treasure hunt. The breeze suddenly picked up, forcing the light cotton shawl off my shoulders. I spun around quickly and grabbed it in time.

I nearly froze at the sight in front of me. Not too far away from me was a tall blond-haired figure, with the cuffs of his beige pants rolled up to his knees. His light blue shirt was also rolled up to his elbows with just a few buttons done up at the bottom, leaving his chest exposed, the edges of his shirt flapping in the wind.

He was laughing, kicking at the water, sending brilliant drops of sparkling beads into the air. He was surrounded by a golden halo, his hair shimmering in the light. He swiveled slightly in my direction, and I could see his chiseled cheekbones and soft tender lips set in a wide grin. I saw a flash of his blue eyes. I gasped at his handsome features, simply gazing at him, enjoying the moment.

He laughed again, bouncing to the water's edge, kicking the frothy bubbles upward. I could now see what he was laughing at. His dog pounced toward him, leaping up in the air to snatch the flying droplets with his teeth. His fur was lit up in a golden halo, so smooth and luxuriously lavish, his long tail swishing in the sunlight.

I sighed happily, my eyes crinkling at the corners, delighted at this wonderful scene. Then, there was an earsplitting crack and I jerked upright, feeling a sharp pain in my neck. The room was dark, the rain streaked angrily down my bedroom window.

"Oh come on! That's so not fair!" I was so disgusted that it was all a dream and deeply disappointed that I woke up so rudely. I glanced upward, scowling, hoping that the Powers That Be would pick up on that message.

I sighed, totally resigned, looking down at my bed, my sketchbook pushed off to the side. A lovely blue pillow festooned with creamy seashells lay beside me along with a well-thumbed Pottery Barn catalog, featuring a seaside theme on its cover.

The deep cobalt blue skies and sandy beaches stretched on for miles in the background. Sun-bleached wooden chairs sat in the foreground stacked with colorful pillows and lanterns beside them, all beckoning to me. If I only had the money...I sighed again.

I creased my forehead as a thought pushed its way to the front. I wonder...The dream had felt so real, as if I could reach out and touch it like I did with this catalog. *Was it a sign? A premonition, perhaps?*

I cast a glance toward Parker who curled up by my feet, the sheets billowing around him. I could swear that he was smiling. His whiskers twitched slightly. He curled up even tighter into a cozy ball, his furry paws covering his nose.

CHAPTER 4

Breakthrough

After going through the disastrous last few weeks, I was looking forward to gym today, eager to take my mind off everything. I quickly changed into my gym clothes and dashed off to the gymnasium, ready to line up. Sensei Jonas watched us stroll in and take our places. I was feeling a bit nervous since he had said he would be bringing in an assistant to help with the final class.

I gulped loudly, feeling my palms sweat nervously. I took a few deep breaths to calm my nerves and nearly choked when I saw his assistant walk through the doors. I swear that my heart skipped a couple of beats and the room seemed to spin around me. If this had been a movie, his theme song would've been something like, "Save Me" from Smallville.

I was familiar with the phrase, "tall drink of water on a hot day," but really hadn't known what it meant...until today. He was strikingly handsome with chiseled features and a strong jaw. His caramel hair was tousled, giving him a casual air. He appeared to be physically fit and slightly tanned, which made his smile even more pronounced, as it revealed his perfectly white teeth.

He literally looked like a walking ad for Abercrombie and Fitch, stunning in every aspect. I had to hold back a moan as he strode across the floor, his eyes twinkling with delight. He appeared supremely confident.

I gulped again loudly, resisting the urge to bite on my fist, holding back my desire to throw myself at him. I tried desperately to pull my eyes away from him as he walked to the front of the class, but I failed miserably.

I fussed with my hair, fixing my bangs and adjusting my ponytail trying to tidy up my appearance, suddenly feeling insecure and very much like a country hick.

He stopped to stand by Sensei Jonas, his feet apart and his hands behind his back.

Sensei Jonas broke my reverie with his shout of "Keske!"

We all promptly slapped our arms to our sides, bringing our feet sharply together. He barked out the next command, "Rei!" and we all bowed in unison.

"Excellent!" he remarked, pleased at our progress in snapping to attention. His voice boomed throughout the gym, surrounding us with a sense of power.

"As you can see, I have an assistant with me today." He gestured toward the tall drink of water. "This is my son, Sensei Ethan." And they nodded to each other. "He will be going around the room to correct your stances, blocks, and strikes."

Sensei Ethan bent over and picked up a large blue pad, as big as my torso, from the floor. He held onto the straps on either side of the pad.

"He will stop in front of you so that you will have the opportunity to kick this shield. Don't worry, it won't hurt him." He smiled broadly as he gestured toward Sensei Ethan.

Sensei Ethan walked to the far end of the first row, five people from my right, holding the pad in front of him. His hips were twisted to the side and he leaned toward the student in front of him. It took all my strength to pull my eyes back toward the front to watch Sensei Jonas lead the class.

"All right, everyone take a step back into the fighting stance with your hips at a forty-five degree angle away from me, with your feet shoulder width apart." He demonstrated and watched all of us follow his motions. "Good! Now raise your hands to shoulder level, arms bent comfortably." He brought up his hands into a fighting posture, his face focused and I instantly felt his demeanor change into a wall of strength.

"This time, twist your hips toward me, turn on the ball of your foot, keeping your knees bent and bring up your right knee." Sensei Jonas brought his leg upward in a swift motion, completely balanced and at ease.

"Now, I want you to push your foot outwards, sharply, kicking with the ball of your foot." He snapped out his foot so hard that I could hear his uniform snap in unison with it.

We all followed his actions to the best of our abilities, some of us leaning to one side awkwardly wind-milling our arms or losing our balance all together.

I focused on the strike, snapping forward, and it felt so strange to me to do this motion.

"Good job everyone! And bring your foot back down to the same spot where you started from.

"Let's do it again, slowly, until you become used to this motion, okay? Here we go." He moved with grace, obviously comfortable with it. I followed his rhythm, feeling awkward and out of place, thinking that I must look like an absolute klutz.

I could feel my face flushing red and felt very self-conscious as I stumbled slightly.

"This time we will do all of this in a single motion. You are going to snap it out quickly on my count. Ready?"

I thought to myself, Aw heck no, I'm so not ready to do this.

He began to count in Japanese, "Ichi!" barking out each number, "Ni!," watching us as he did the kicks along with us, "San!"

Suddenly Sensei Ethan was right in front of me with the blue shield. I faltered, startled by his presence. "Sorry," I muttered. He looked at me with his hazel eyes and I nearly melted on the spot.

"That's okay. Go ahead and kick as hard as you can," he said smiling.

I felt my heart jump at the sound of his silky voice. His gaze was smoldering and I had to blink to break our eye contact. I focused on the center of the pad, took a quick breath, and kicked it feebly, closing one eye, afraid to hurt him.

He grinned wider. "Kick harder."

My breath was a bit shaky. I threw all of my weight into it this time, feeling a satisfying thunk as the pad gave way beneath my foot. Wow, it felt great! I did it again, feeling more confident.

"Yes! That's it! Keep it up!" His eyes twinkled as he looked at me, delighted at my progress.

It was then that I dimly realized just how attracted I was to him. I was drawn to him, sinking into his eyes and suddenly was acutely aware that he was staring at me intently.

I quickly looked down, blushing fiercely, certain he could see how red I was, and kicked hard as I could at the pad, again and again.

"Good job," he said, winking at me so quickly that I wasn't sure if really happened. Then he walked over to the next student beside me.

We switched feet, now kicking with our left foot on Sensei Jonas's counts. I worked as hard as I could, trying to make my kicks look as good as his, which would've taken a miracle.

After several minutes of delivering front kicks, we took a break as we listened to Sensei Jonas. "The kick that you worked is excellent for striking the knees, the stomach or groin area. Remember to bring your foot back quickly otherwise your opponent can grab it and force you off balance."

Good point. I'd have to remember that.

"Watch how hard I kick this shield." He gestured for Sensei Ethan to move toward him with the shield. He reacted quickly and extremely fast with a loud thwack! The force of his explosive kick pushed Sensei Ethan back a foot or two. I stood there stunned, pretty sure that my jaw was sitting on my chest.

Neither one of them flinched nor batted an eye as if this was an everyday occurrence.

I could feel my body curling inwards in fear at the sight of his kick.

He turned to face us as he spoke. "This time we will work on high blocks. Stay in your fighting stance with your hips at an angle." He brought up his hands in a defensive mode, very much like what a boxer would do.

"As you raise your right arm, cross it in front of your body to protect your chest then bring it upward just above your head. Remember to keep your arm bent with the fleshy part facing outwards."

As he demonstrated the block, Sensei Ethan moved in and did a slow motion strike toward his father's head.

Sensei Jonas continued speaking about protecting our face and head. "Be careful about having your arm too close to your face. If the opponent were to hit your arm, you could end up hitting your own face and also leave the top of your head exposed to a strike. If you move your arm too high above your head, then your face will be vulnerable to strikes as well."

Sensei Ethan would feign an attack toward his father's head to demonstrate the differences.

"Okay, I want everyone to follow my motions," Sensei Jonas said.

I watched him carefully, feeling like a duck out of water. My arms felt like they were on strike, unwilling to coordinate themselves.

Nonetheless, I concentrated on trying it out, knowing that it may very well save my life.

Sensei Ethan moved down the first row again, this time moving toward us slowly as he mimicked an overhead strike. I could see him out of the corner of my eye, my heart beating faster the closer he moved in my direction.

I moved my arms in time to Sensei Jonas's counts, watching him move so fluidly. Then it was my turn, I sucked in my breath in anticipation of Sensei Ethan's overhead strikes.

The pressure was immense and I felt like I was suddenly in the spotlight in front of hundreds of people.

He raised his arm toward my head and I responded by bringing up my arm in an attempt to block it.

"That's it." He spoke gently. "And again. Good. And with the other arm now."

I switched sides, bringing up my left arm, trying to deflect the strike. As I brought it up, he caught it and held it there. His fingers felt warm on my skin as he turned my arm outwards, correcting the position. I tried hard not to react to his touch.

"Be sure to twist your arm like this so that this part is exposed, not the bony part." He ran his fingers down the length of my arm, causing shivers to run down my spine.

I held my breath for fear that I might say something incredibly stupid. He looked into my eyes again and my heart went nuts. All I could do was nod in response.

"Now, let's try it again." He stepped back, briefly watching the motions as I practiced the blocks. "Yes! You got it!" he said before he continued down the row.

We worked on our blocks for several more minutes and took another break. This time we sat down cross-legged on the cold floor as we watched the two instructors demonstrate various self-defense techniques, moving back and forth like a well-rehearsed tango.

"You can use any object to defend yourself, such as a hairbrush to rake across their face or a hard book to block hits.

"Here's a simple trick to distract someone if they happen to grab the front of your shirt and you can move your arms." Sensei Jonas motioned for his son to grab onto his lapels. "What you do is cup your hands, creating a pocket of air.

"Then you bring your hands upward and clap them over their ears quickly." His hands snapped up on both sides of Sensei's Ethan's head and made a cupping motion over his ears. Sensei Ethan promptly released his grip and stepped away.

"As you see, he let go from the strike of my hands. The pressure is intense and loud for most people. I did not use full force here, just enough to startle him. On the streets, you would use full force, as hard as you can.

"All right, everyone grab a partner or form a group with three people and practice this technique, slowly and gently. Remember, anything you do to your partner, they will be doing it to you too."

I stood up and went toward Amanda who was sitting a few feet away from me. "Hi, Amanda. Want to be my partner?"

She smiled in earnest. "Sure!"

I trusted Amanda and felt confident around her. We tried the cupping motion with our hands, rolling them over each other's ears to get used to the feeling. Within minutes of trying it out, Sensei Ethan was by our sides, watching us. "Very nice, ladies." His voice sounded sincere.

He reached for me, bringing his hands on both sides of my neck. His hands were so warm and inviting that I nearly leaned into them.

"What's your name?" he asked.

"Jessie," I replied feeling very shy at that moment.

He turned toward Amanda. "And your name?"

She quickly answered him.

"Okay, Amanda. I want you to curl your hands like this, thus cupping the ear as much as possible. We want to trap the air in there."

I could feel his hands slowly roll over my ears as he demonstrated the motions. My mouth suddenly went very dry.

"I see," said Amanda as she watched him carefully.

My hearing aids suddenly emitted a piercing squeal from the feedback caused by his hands coming in contact with them.

I immediately felt ashamed and promptly apologized, my eyes starting to water, tears threatening to form. I quickly looked downwards so that he wouldn't see.

"It's my fault, Jessie, not yours," he said apologetically, pulling his hands away. His fingers traced the edges of my jaw as he withdrew.

My ears suddenly felt cold and naked.

"Jessie, it's your turn," he said.

I turned toward Amanda and tried the technique carefully.

"That's it! You got it!" He smiled and ambled over to observe another group.

Sensei Jonas called us to the front and we all promptly lined up, standing with our hands behind our backs in a listening stance.

"Great job everyone! I'm very pleased with how well some of you have progressed. Sensei Ethan and I have been watching all of you very closely today and I believe that we picked one of you as top of the class based on dedication, focus, and hard work."

Sensei Ethan leaned over to his father's ear and whispered to him.

"When I call your name, please come forward."

I listened, curious as to whom it could be. I had no idea that they were going to choose anyone as top student.

Both he and Sensei Ethan looked my way and I assumed it was Amanda or Donna who were standing on either side of me. "Jessie, please come forward."

I stood frozen, shocked that my name was called and I wondered if I imagined it.

He gestured at me to stand beside him. I was shaking, nervous and dazed. I walked shyly to the front to stand by his side. He placed a hand on my shoulder in respect. "Jessie was chosen because she has demonstrated a remarkable ability to follow instructions, shown strength, confidence, and has proven that she is a true martial artist." He clapped his hand on my shoulder with pride and shook my hand.

I looked out at the sea of my classmates, their faces etched with shock and disbelief. Sensei Ethan reached forward and eagerly clasped my hand in his, pumping it with enthusiasm.

Sensei Jonas turned to face me and said, "Arigato." The words flowed off his tongue. He bowed to me and I bowed back. Still utterly dazed, I started to go back to my spot but he stopped me. "Jessie, you are welcome to stand by our side and bow to the class. "Keske!" We all snapped to attention. "Rei!" He bowed as he dismissed the class.

I was in absolute awe as I bowed to them, feeling so strange to be in this position. I ran my fingers through my hair, nervously wondering what to do next as the class dispersed, leaving in groups, chattering amongst themselves, some whispering and looking over their shoulders at me.

I was about to walk toward the changing room when Sensei Ethan called my name, striding toward me with a dazzling smile.

"Jessie, wait—before you go." He reached out to touch my arm gently. "I have something for you." He presented me with a card with logo of a karate student doing a sidekick and the words, "Kenpo Karate," beside it. There was also an address, phone number and two email addresses beneath it.

"Have you considered taking Karate?" he asked, his eyes beckoning me.

I stammered, "N—No. It never crossed my mind. I'm still shocked that you picked me as top of the class."

His hand curled around my arm. "Believe me, you earned it."

"Wow. Thank you. That means a lot to me."

"Would you please consider it? You have the talent within you. I can see it."

I got the impression that he was being completely honest with me.

"But I can't afford it," I said, dismayed.

"The first month is free, and that includes the uniform."

My heart beat wildly at the thought of being with him, excited at the prospect of actually becoming a full-fledged student. My mind swirled with the possibilities and it felt right.

"I would love to." I smiled at him, feeling giddy. "I'm looking forward to it."

"Please email me if you have any questions. Again, congratulations. I'm proud of you." He extended his right arm and we shook hands, not really wanting to let go.

His father called him. "Ethan, let's go."

"Bye," he said as he turned and walked away from me.

I floated back to the changing room on a cloud, blissfully happy, clutching his card to my chest. As soon as I opened the door, all eyes were on me.

Amanda and Erica were instantly by my side, squealing, "He's so cute!"

"Way to go, Jessie!"

They congratulated me with pats on my back and broad smiles.

"Thanks," was all I could say.

I could feel the eyes of my teammates on me, namely Donna, Buffy, and Kathy, shaking their heads in disbelief, whispering to each other as I sat down to change.

CHAPTER 5

Trust

Several of the other students took their own sweet time as they strode back to the changing room after gym class. Some of them giggled loudly, while others discussed what to do after school. It was a mix of voices that blurred together in a rush of noise.

Feeling euphoric, like after a good basketball game, I barely heard the cacophony of my classmates in the crowded changing room, their voices overlapping loudly, all sitting beneath the low line of hooks along the wall. Peering under the bench, I grabbed my black gym bag pulling it out to sit in front of me and started to pull off my gym shoes and socks, tossing them into the bag. I quickly stripped off my shorts, turned around, grabbed my jeans off the hook, and tugged them on. Something nagged at the back of my mind. I kept getting the odd feeling that something was not right.

I shrugged my shoulders and went back to getting dressed, yanking off my drenched T-shirt and pulling on a long sleeved shirt over my head. I turned around again, reaching for the hook when it finally dawned on me what was missing.

The room seemed to spin out of control as I realized what had happened. Gasping frantically, I searched through my bag, looked under the bench. My eyes scanned the room, checking out all of the hooks on the walls. "No, it can't be happening..." I placed my hand on my chest as tears suddenly welled up in my eyes.

I heard a distant voice as I sat down. "Jessie. What's wrong?" It was Stephanie, looking at me, concern etched on her face.

I was barely able to speak, afraid my voice would break. "My shirt! It's gone."

Looking puzzled, Stephanie said, "What shirt?"

Anger bubbled up in my chest, hot with intense rage. "You know what I mean! The long sleeved red and purple one that I always wear—it's gone!"

Her eyes opened wide, shocked. "Don't worry, Jessie. I'll help you look for it." She got up and walked around the changing room as the rest of the group continued to chatter, ignoring her. The room was almost empty. Some of them were looking over their shoulders as they left. Stephanie looked everywhere without any success and I felt a sense of despair wash over me.

"Come on, we gotta go or we'll be late for the next class," Stephanie said as she tugged on my arm gently, encouraging me to go with her.

"No, you go on ahead. Thanks for your help though," I replied numbly. I grabbed my gym bag, gathered my books into my arms, and stormed out toward the office for Phys-Ed. Eyes blazing with anger, I knocked on the door beside the sign that displayed the letters, "Physical Education Department." The door jerked open, revealing an office filled with sports manuals, anatomy charts displayed on the wall, and various equipment tucked away in the corner.

The desk was covered with piles of paperwork, a red pen sat on top ready to be used. Mrs. Stewart sat in her chair, listening on the phone, replying with short remarks, "Uh huh. Sure, that's fine." She glanced up at me, holding up her finger to her lips then pointing at the phone. As usual, she wore her tracksuit, dove gray with white stripes running down the sides. Her hair was equally as dull, cut in an unflattering style and much too short for her lean face.

"Yeah, listen, I have to go, there's a student here waiting for me." She hung up and turned around to face me squarely. "Yes? What can I do for you?"

I gripped the doorframe with my free hand, holding back a mix of emotions from rage to disbelief and I quickly declared, "My shirt! It's been stolen!"

"Are you sure?" Her eyebrows creased together in concern. "It wasn't misplaced?"

Restraining myself from yelling, I said, "Yes, I'm sure! I looked everywhere!"

Sighing, she crossed her arms in front of her chest. "Maybe someone grabbed it by mistake?" She looked at me, sensing my distress and continued. "Don't worry about it. It may show up later, okay?"

Frustrated, I threw up my hand, exasperated by her lame responses. "No, it's not okay! You don't understand, it was stolen!" Tears started to form in my eyes, blurring her figure into blobs of colors.

Growing impatient and obviously trying to dismiss me, she replied, "You know what? It's just a shirt. You can always buy another one." She stood with her hand on the doorframe, clearly unaware of the significance of the shirt.

It was my favorite shirt. One that my brother had given to me before he left to work up North. It meant a lot to me.

Shocked by her attitude, I abruptly turned around and nearly ran down the hallway, past the walls decorated with sports posters and signup sheets. I slowed down and walked briskly, past the lockers, fuming and barely noticing the glances from the other students as I pushed by them.

I muttered angrily to myself, "Stupid crowds." I found myself in front of the principal's office, desperate to talk to someone with authority.

The secretary in front of me broke through my stormy thoughts with her dry voice, sounding bored. "No dear, he's not in right now. Is there anything I can do to help?" She was a little older than my mother, glasses hanging on a chain around her neck, her hair held up in a clip at the back with tufts of hair peeking out.

"I wanted to report a theft," I said brusquely.

Surprise flickered across her face as I spoke. "Are you sure?" she asked. "That's a serious accusation."

I thought sardonically, *What is this? Clue?* I rolled my eyes exasperated. "Yes, I know it's serious, that's why I'm here!" I said as I thumped my books on the counter.

She reached over to a pile of papers, grabbed a form, pen poised in the air. "All right, tell me what happened."

I described the shirt in detail, explaining that I had it in the changing room during gym class.

She looked up at me, shaking her head. "Tell you what, I'll file this report but I honestly don't think it will help. Thefts are a frequent occurrence around here." She spoke again as an afterthought. "In the future, I would keep items of value in the locker." Her voice faded away as I dimly realized the truth, I'd never see it again.

"Hang on. There are no lockers in the changing room. What am I supposed to do? Change in the hallway?" I asked sarcastically.

She continued to speak to me but I ignored her comments as I walked away feeling hopeless. I wandered down the hallway, shuffling my feet, lost in thought.

Who would do this to me? I wondered. *And why?* My head was filled with impossible questions that I couldn't answer.

I looked up at the clock in the hallway, not caring that I had missed a class. *Great*, I thought dully. I have to wait all afternoon before the bus picks me up.

I walked past a public phone near the front doors and an idea popped into my head. I took a few steps back, rummaged through my bag for some change and tried dialing home, turning up the volume. It rang continuously and I hung up after the fifth ring. *What about Grandpa?* I punched in his number, frantically trying to come up with a plausible excuse for calling him.

He picked it up on the third ring. "Hello?"

"Hi, Grandpa. Can you come and pick me up from school?" I asked meekly, crossing my fingers and hoping he would say yes.

Upon hearing the concern in his voice, I felt a twinge of guilt for calling him. "Sure I can do that, it's not a problem. Are you all right?"

I sighed with relief and boldly lied through my teeth. "Just a headache, Grandpa. I don't feel like going to class this afternoon."

"Hang on, honey. I'll be there in a few minutes and meet you out front."

I hung up and went straight to my locker, stuffing my books into my backpack, pulling on my boots and jacket, feeling its thinness without my shirt.

I walked to the lobby, looking out the large glass windows, and bounced on my feet impatiently. It seemed like an eternity until I finally saw his blue station wagon crawl toward the curb, its tires crunching in the snow. Breathless, I yanked opened the door, threw my backpack on the floor, and quickly yanked on my seatbelt.

"Thanks, Gramps," I said, forcing a smile, hoping he didn't see through it.

"Don't worry about it, sweetie." He looked at me concerned. "Are you sure you're all right?"

Quietly, I said, "It's nothing, just a bad headache."

"I hope it's not the flu. That has been going around lately."

We drove in silence for a few minutes until he cleared his throat. "You seem cold, Jessie. Didn't you dress warmly for today?" His eyes assessed my jacket.

My throat suddenly constricted with fresh sadness making it hard to breathe. I mumbled and looked out the window, away from his gaze. "Guess I forgot."

"Oh well, try to add another layer or two next time. It'll help keep you warm." He clicked on the radio and soft jazz music filled the car.

Feeling a little bit more at ease and comforted by the familiar music, I leaned my head against the cool window and closed my eyes.

After what seemed like a very long ride, possibly the longest in my life, we finally rumbled to a stop in front of my house. I grabbed my backpack from the floor, fingers on the door handle. "Thanks for the ride, I appreciate it."

"Wait, are you sure you don't want someone to stay with you?"

I looked at him as he spoke, my heart breaking. "Nah, I'll just make a cup of tea and go to my room. It's fine, really."

"All right, honey. Get some sleep okay?" He smiled, his eyes crinkling at the corners.

"Okay, bye!" I scrambled out of the car and went up the stairs to the front door. I turned around and waved, watching him drive away down the lane.

Feeling an overwhelming sense of despair, I rushed up the stairs to my room, dumped everything on the floor and crawled up on the bench beneath the window. I clutched a pillow to my chest as the sobs broke through. Intense grief filled my body, painfully and uncontrollably.

I sat on the bench, staring blankly at the sky as the sun sank into the horizon, shadows moving across my room, completely unaware of time.

I found myself standing in the snow, walking through it, and not noticing its coldness. It felt strange as I admired the sparkling surface. I strolled past several buildings that were tall and vast, unusual in their design, seemingly ancient. They appeared to be made of shimmering smooth marble, white and glistening in the light. Tiny crystals embedded in the surface, refracting the light a thousand ways like quartz.

I stood before an enormous domed building shaped like a cathedral. As I stepped toward the door, it disappeared, and I found myself inside the room, staring up at a vast arched ceiling that seemed to sparkle. Its sculpted beams met in the center. Smooth, giant pillars lined the hallways with rooms on either side. Each entrance was covered with an elaborate archway. It was glorious, full of warm flickering light, each room softly lit.

One room in particular caught my eye with its random flickering light that cast long shadows out into the hallway. I moved forward, stepping softly near the door. I cautiously peered in around the edge of the doorway, nearly blinded by the bright light. Along the walls in the room were rows and rows of long and angular prisms that resembled quartz crystals. They sprouted from the wall, nearly reaching the ceiling. Many of them were the same size as my hand, some smaller than others, and some much larger. They were neither factory-made nor carved by hand. Rather they appeared to have grown naturally from the quartz within the walls. The crystals were long with smooth sides, semi clear, and filled with shimmering reflective fragments that resembled colorful, glittering sand floating inside.

Absolutely curious, I leaned closer and was surprised to discover a glowing light in the center, similar to a flame. I pulled back, looked at the others around me, and saw that nearly all of them contained a flickering light. I stood there, perplexed, wondering what they were, mesmerized by their illumination when Parker shimmered into existence beside me, his golden skin luminous in this room.

He nodded his head toward me. "May I offer insight?" he asked gently.

I gaped at him, still stunned by his sudden appearance. "Yes, please do. These crystals are highly unusual, beautiful to look at but I don't know what they mean." Come to think of it, this whole scenario was rather unusual.

He gestured in the direction of the crystals with a broad sweep of his arm. "These are life force crystals of everyone here."

I blinked for a moment processing this information then stopped at the word, "here." Where was here?

Speaking softly, he continued with his explanation. "See how some are brighter than others?" He pointed to a small one just off to my left that glowed so strongly the light bounced around me like a disco ball. "They have hope and remain strong and vibrant."

He moved to a dimmer crystal. Even though it was bigger than the others, the flame inside struggled to glow. "This one has lost hope and is becoming weaker." His eyes seemed sad as he leaned in to gaze at it, his face shadowed from the dull crystal. It sputtered from time to time, trying desperately to glow but seemed to be out of energy.

"Perhaps you would like a moment to ponder the meaning of this?" he said, looking around the room. I nodded as I took it all in, wondering what he meant and what the purpose of these crystals was.

"Let hope be your guide. Find inspiration in the most unlikely places," he uttered cryptically as he started to shimmer once again, his voice fading.

Lovely. Now I just had to figure out what it meant. I leaned down and stared at the crystals, feeling their pull as I watched the multi-hued light dance within them, scattering their beams in every direction.

One of them seemed to glow brighter as I watched it, and I had to squint to against its brightness. I turned away for a moment, bringing up my hand against the glare.

When I opened my eyes again, I was staring at Parker, sound asleep on the bench. I reached out to touch his fur, not believing that he was real. Upon feeling its softness, I sat back, perplexed at what had just happened.

CHAPTER 6

Full Moon

As I opened my eyes in the morning, the room felt colder than usual. I shivered as I yanked off the covers to look out the window. I was stunned at the amount of snow blanketing our front yard. It created a serene and surreal landscape. The snow was blindingly bright, and I had to raise my hand to cover my eyes for a moment to reduce the glare.

It looked as if it had snowed all night long, never stopping, and draped every conceivable surface with thick, heavy layers of snow. As I admired the scenery, large chunks of snow fell through the branches, creating a slushy avalanche. I could see a long line of deer tracks wandering through the field. Apparently the deer were in search of food, munching on the bits of stalks sticking up through the snow.

Cool. I quickly ran down the stairs to see if there were any sticky notes on the counter in the kitchen. Mom knew that I had trouble hearing the radio announcements for school closures and she would often leave a note letting me know what they said. I spun around, looked under the table, thinking it had fallen off the counter. "Nope, nothing. Dang."

Resigned, I glumly went back up the stairs, searched through my closet and drawers for warm clothes, and marched into the washroom to get ready.

I managed to find a muffin and have a sip of orange juice before I stepped outside, bracing myself for the blast of cold air. Pulling my scarf more snuggly around my face and ears, I trudged through the deep snow. It was eerily silent as I made my way down the lane, which seemed much longer than usual. The air smelled fresh and crisp.

My boots felt huge and sluggish from the heavy snow. I bent down gathering it up into a tight ball. The snow was the perfect consistency for making snowballs, and I just couldn't resist trying it out. I tossed one at a nearby tree as I passed it, hitting it dead center.

I waited for perhaps ten minutes for the bus to arrive. It came to a slushy stop in front of the mailbox. I pounced up the stairs, slung my backpack on the seat, and sat down, barely glancing at the other kids behind me.

A few minutes into the ride, while stopping to pick up several more students, I heard the guys behind me taunting me, trying to get my attention.

I ignored them to the best of my abilities, closed my eyes, and gripped the seat tightly with my hands, my knuckles turning white from the effort, as I took long, deep breaths.

They were awfully persistent today, determined to drive me nuts. After what seemed like an eternity, I heard them snorting with stifled laughter. Geez Louise, what were they up to now? I gripped the seat even tighter.

Someone tapped me on the shoulder. *Sigh...it's never going to end, is it?* I hissed at them. "What?" I turned my head and opened my eyes. "Oh for the love of..."

Across the seat to my left, hidden from the bus driver, was a full moon, courtesy of Nathan, who was chortling, with his pants around his knees.

A surge of heat filled my face, partly from shame and anger. I flicked my eyes toward the bus driver who didn't even notice what was happening. Then I did a quick scan on either side of me. They were all snickering and pointing their fingers toward me. No one came to my defense. I slouched deeper into the seat, turned away from them, and stared out the window. I could hear them guffawing now, giving each other a high fives.

Finally, we arrived at school and I scampered out of the bus as quickly as I could.

They yelled at me as I pounded down the stairs, "Hey Jessie! Did you know there's a full moon tonight?" Their laughter filled the bus as I left.

Honestly, it was embarrassing having to take the bus, being subjected to this type of ridicule day after day. It was a form of never ending torture. I couldn't wait to learn how to drive and get to school on my own.

I picked up the FM system on my way to my locker, checking that it was working before snatching it out of the charging station. Once I reached the locker, I stripped off my wet boots, laced up my pink sneakers, grabbed my books, and dashed off to class. The classroom was huge and filled with shelves of art supplies. Elaborate posters decorated the walls and a kiln sat in the back corner, surrounded by a chain-link fence. Several large sinks stood by the wall and long desks sat in the center of the room, arranged in the shape of an elongated horseshoe.

Mr. Brown already sat at his desk, flipping through sheets of papers, with a pen in one hand. I plunked down the microphone—a small blue box with a clear loop attached to the top of it—beside him. He reached for it and placed it around his neck.

"Ah, good morning Jessie!" he said with a smile, his receding brown hair exposing a shiny forehead, his nose scattered with light freckles. He wore a beige pin-striped long-sleeved shirt that was rolled up the elbows, with various pencils sitting in his pocket.

His name never failed to amuse me. How often do I have a teacher whose name matched the subject matter they taught? The irony of it was, in my opinion, hilarious. I smiled at that thought as I made my way to toward the tables.

There were still a few minutes before class started so I pulled out my sketchbook and started working on some ideas for an upcoming poster contest. I moved the drawing of an oasis I had done earlier off to the side while I did some sketching.

Several other students milled around me, finding their seats and slamming their books on the table, breaking my focus. I looked up to see Sandy pull out a chair and sit down on my right side as Danny sat on my left. Great. Bookended by the famous twins. I thought darkly, dreading the conversation that was bound to come up.

Sandy had quite the reputation at school for being promiscuous, preferring older men. She had a provocative personality, exuding confidence in every way possible, from her flashy clothes, to the sexy smile and attitude to match. Her curly brown hair, perfect make up, large eye-catching earrings, and of course a low-cut sweater, made her look as if she'd stepped out of a glossy fashion magazine. It was obvious that they were rolling in money and had no qualms about publicly displaying it.

Danny, on the other hand, seemed much more shy and acted insecure, but I always got the impression that it was all an act, a plot devised between the two of them to drive me insane. They clearly enjoyed playing all sorts of jokes on me, particularly in regards to dumb, blonde jokes.

Sandy was the type of person who would steal your boyfriend or go behind your back and say the most derogatory remarks you ever heard. She would do everything in her power to make life miserable for anyone who got in her way and then deny it, suddenly acting angelic.

I couldn't even count how many times she had borrowed something of mine and, of course, stupid me, she never returned it, claiming that she had never done such a thing. She knew how to be cunning and get away with it. I could easily see her, in my mind, as the devil, complete with horns and a pitchfork.

I bent my head lower, concentrating on my sketching, hoping to avoid any sort of interaction with them.

Mr. Brown was walking around the class with a clipboard in his hand, taking attendance. He stopped behind me, looking over my shoulder. "Jessie, that's a great sketch!" He beamed, pointing at my drawing of the palm trees surrounded by a deep orange sunset. "You know what? You should consider doing a silk screen of that onto shirts. It's such a fun design!" he quipped enthusiastically.

I nodded, remembering Robin's Moose sketch, looking forward to seeing his design on shirts. "Thanks Mr. Brown. I'll think about." I smiled back, pleasantly surprised by his remark.

I went back to my sketch, tapping my pencil on the pad, trying to come up some more ideas. I could feel Sandy tugging at my sleeve, snapping me out my thoughts. Irritated, I looked in her direction, waiting with bated breath for her next prank. "Yes, Sandy?" I responded as calmly as I could muster between gritted teeth.

She had the look of an innocent girl when I knew dark thoughts lurked beneath those pampered eyes. "Say, Jessie, I was wondering what you were planning on doing tonight?"

Her question startled me as it was so out of character for her. She never did anything remotely nice to me unless she had an ulterior motive. I stammered, caught off guard. "What? Oh, I don't know, homework most likely. I still have to finish the essay for Mrs. Evans that's due this week."

She barely batted an eye as if expecting that response. *Weird. What was she up to now?*

"Oh, yeah! I forgot about that, thanks for reminding me!" she said as she reached for one of my pens.

I placed my hands on top of them. "Excuse me? What'cha doing?"

Despite her benign behavior, I still didn't trust her.

"Please? I ran out and I need a pen," she asked imploringly, lowering my defenses slightly.

"Why can't Danny give you one of his?" I jerked my head in his direction. He was watching us blankly, his face revealing no sinister motive.

"He's down to his last one," she replied meekly.

I sighed deeply. "Fine, but I want it back before you leave this class." I gave her one that I knew was running low on ink, still not entirely convinced she was being honest.

"Thanks," she said as she reached out for it.

I went back to my sketchbook, my hand moving across the page as I drew more images until Danny elbowed me in my arm. *What now? Is this a tag team thing or something?"* I turned to glare at him. His eyes stared back at me, unblinking. I had to suppress a shiver for his eyes revealed not a speck of emotion. It was as if the lights were on but nobody was home.

He primarily kept to himself and would often smile at me in the hallway, offering a polite hello from time to time.

He smiled at me. "Hi," he said slightly apprehensive, holding onto his books tightly. He wore a dark blue sweater over a lighter blue shirt, not quite tucked into his pants. His dark hair was rumpled and wavy, falling into his eyes, his face still pudgy, having not quite grown out of the baby fat yet.

Between the two of them, I never knew what they had hidden up their sleeves and I always felt guarded around them. "Hey, Danny." I smiled back, being as polite as possible.

He continued to stare unwaveringly at me, making me nervous and somewhat uncomfortable. "I love your eyes. They are so blue," he said.

"Uh, thanks Danny. That's kind of you to say." Our conversation felt so wrong, so out of place.

He was about to speak again when the bell pealed loudly and Mr. Brown stood in front of us to begin the class. He walked across the floor, carrying a large stack of huge sheets for doing charcoal sketches and began passing them around. "All right everyone. Listen up. We are going to be doing charcoal sketches today so I want you to roll up your sleeves since this can get messy.

"But first I will demonstrate what I want you to work on today." He dragged an upright easel closer to the center of the room and swiftly drew several three-dimensional shapes on the sheet, talking about shading techniques.

The class went by quickly as we all practiced our strokes, pressing the charcoal sticks on the sheets of paper in front of us, creating a smudgy mess of fingerprints around the edges.

As I went over to the sink to wash my hands, Sandy passed the pen to me. "Thanks Jessie. Guess I didn't need it today after all."

"Guess not," I said as I plucked it from her fingers, surprised that she even gave it back to me.

On my way out, I stopped briefly to gather the microphone from Mr. Brown. He nodded politely at me as he passed it over to me.

I had always found Mr. Brown to one of my most level-headed teachers this year. He was obviously talented but he was also polite and very patient with everyone. He seemed to appreciate our creative styles regardless of our skill levels and had a tendency to remain calm in what could be a chaotic class at times. He was one of the few teachers who tolerated using the microphone, no questions asked, unless it was turned off, of course.

We went our separate ways until lunchtime, when we gathered in the auditorium. I wove through the crow, searching for a place to sit and found a spot at one of the benches. I dumped my lunch bag on top of the long table and sat down next to Amanda and Erica, both who were friendly to me but not necessarily close, more casual acquaintances. They were smart and independent which suited me fine. At least we could have more interesting conversations.

Amanda's long blond hair was pulled up into a simple ponytail. She wore a soft yellow sweater and indigo jeans. Erica had her raven black hair tucked away in a clip, a few tufts sticking up from the top. She was wearing a creamy white and green striped pullover, complimented by a long green scarf, and black jeans. The two of them were flipping through a textbook, muttering to each other and exchanging puzzled glances.

While munching on a carrot stick, looking over Amanda's shoulder, I could see Danny and Sandy hanging out with their super preppy group, three tables down from us, watching me casually. They tipped their heads toward each other once in a while as if hatching their diabolical plan. I could feel their eyes on me and immediately felt my face flush warmly, embarrassed that I was obviously the source of their conversation.

I still had a nagging suspicion in the back of my mind that those two were up to something. Over the past year they had proven to be untrustworthy, even though they remained popular, with loads of friends at their beck and call. As far as I could tell, their pranks were a way of dealing with boredom. It was the thrill of the chase that appealed to them.

Amanda was tapping on my shoulder. "Jess? Jessie!"

My focus snapped back to Amanda's face, her eyebrows creased in the middle, waiting for an answer.

"Huh? Say that again."

She sighed, a bit frustrated that she had to repeat herself. "I said, are you interested in coming with us to the audition this week?"

Boy, I must've missed a good portion of the conversation to be this confused. "What audition?"

"Didn't you know that the school is putting on the play *Grease?*" Amanda became more animated as she spoke while Erica nodded her head enthusiastically.

I nearly gagged on the juice I was sipping, coughing, my voice momentarily hoarse. "Did you just say *Grease?*"

"Yeah! Oh come on, it'll be fun. It would mean a lot to us if you came with us. Please?" begged Amanda.

"Please?" chimed in Erica.

Looking at these two with their pleading eyes and bouncy enthusiasm, I couldn't help myself and gave in, kinda. "Fine. I'll think about it. But no promises." I wagged my finger at them, suddenly terrified that I had committed myself to this challenge with no way out.

Amanda and Erica clapped their hands with glee, their hair bouncing in tune with their bubbly gestures. Mentally, I was praying that I didn't get trapped into making a gigantic fool of myself.

My heart was pounding in fear and excitement as I smiled at them.

"Oops, where did the time go?" exclaimed Erica as she peeked at her watch. "Our next class will start soon."

Amanda waved as she got up, gathering her lunch bag. "See you later Jessie!"

I stood up along with them and strolled out of the auditorium, my mind racing with multiple thoughts about the upcoming audition and the twin's odd behavior toward me.

I was sitting in Mrs. Evan's advanced English class, without any reference notes in front of me, trying to follow her voice as she read an excerpt from William Blake. It drove me nuts when she would do this without providing a copy for me to follow since I often missed a portion of what was spoken.

She knew full well that it wasn't easy for me to hear her quiet voice even when she used the microphone. The class was often noisy with the scraping of the chairs on the floor, the relentless tapping of someone's pencil on their desk, the sharp flipping noise from someone turning the page over in their binder, and the constant hum of the AC in the background. Plus her glossy black high-heeled shoes were unbelievably loud as she walked across the floor, sounding more like hollow gunshots with every step she took.

Today she looked the part of an uptight librarian with her long brown hair tucked into a bun at the top of her head and her lips pinched. She wore a soft gray blouse with a silver-gray tie decorated with white polka dots and a black pencil skirt.

I really had to strain to make out the words and was immensely relived when she uttered the last word as she slapped the book closed and placed it on her desk.

"Now then. I have a special surprise for all of you today." Mrs. Evans smiled as she clapped her hands together, pleased with the announcement.

Curious, I perked up and sat a bit straighter in my chair, pen poised over my notes.

"Your assignment for this month will be writing to your Pen Pals from the province of Calgary." A murmur rose noticeably in the class along with the odd groan from a few students.

"A friend of mine is a teacher at one of the high schools in Calgary and he has agreed to exchange letters with our class. Here is the first batch." She reached for a large stack of letters and started placing them on our desks as she walked around the room.

"There is no need to worry about postage stamps or envelopes since you will be corresponding with your pen pal by email. Each student's address is located at the top of each letter and they are for you only. I do not want anyone exchanging pen pals since these students were matched up based on your personalities."

I looked down at the printed letter in front of me and spotted the name in the upper corner. "Randy." It sounded like a name for a Rodeo cowboy.

Mrs. Evans continued to drone on as she walked around, plunking down the sheets. "Their last names have not been included in these letters for privacy reasons and I am to ask you to do the same if possible.

"For your interest, I have a posted a class photo of these students on the back wall with a list of their names below." She never even got to finish her sentence since there was a sudden stampede to get a good look at their pen pals.

Immensely curious, I, too, went to view the glossy eight-by-ten image, searching the list of names, running my fingers across them until I hit his name. *No way! Is this a joke?* He was by far, the most good-looking guy in the entire class. He stood in the back row and stood out from the group with his tall stature, thick shoulders, and tousled black hair. He had the most adorable dimples, a square cut jaw, and perfect white teeth. He looked like a football player, a guy that everyone would want to hang out with. He could easily be voted the next Prom King.

Sandy stood beside me with her jaw dropped as she spotted my finger on his name, her eyes flitting back and forth between me and Randy. I could swear that she was practically drooling and plotting her next move. She promptly clamped her mouth shut, flung her hair over her shoulder with a "Hmph!" before stomping back to her desk.

I was elated, nearly floating on clouds back to my seat. Wow. Never in my life had I been blessed with enough luck to have a friend as good looking as Randy. I couldn't wait to get home and start typing a response to him.

The bell rang and I quickly shoved the letter into my notebook, stopping to pick up the microphone from Mrs. Evans on the way out.

As soon as I was in the hallway, I was immediately saddled with Sandy prompting me for more information about Randy. I rolled my eyes. *How predictable. Her fingers had been practically caressing the photo.*

I kept walking, determined to ignore her, which was difficult since it was like having a puppy constantly nip at my ankles. I sighed deeply, hoping that she would go away and lust after someone else, but nooo.

"What?" I said after a few minutes of her nagging me, constantly pulling at my sleeve saying, "Please?" like a lost puppy dog. Bambi didn't hold candle to her. I softened, letting my guard down a smidgen, which was a mistake.

"Oh come on. Do you really think he would want to talk to you after seeing your picture?"

I was stunned as if she had slapped me in the face. "Excuse me? You heard what Mrs. Evans said, no exchanges!" I spat out and stormed away, utterly full of hot rage.

The rest of the afternoon classes were comparatively boring and I was glad it was over. When the last bell rang, I dashed out to put my equipment away, pulled on my boots and jacket, and searched for my ride amongst the long row of yellow buses lined up.

By the time I got on, it was already quite full and there were a few spots left near the back. "Crappity, crap, crap!" I really hated sitting back there. It was always the same group of Neanderthals who reeked of cigarette smoke, wore dark clothes, had shoddy, greasy hair and immature attitudes.

I dreaded the ride back home for it would seem like hours next to these buffoons. Placing my backpack in my lap, I glared out the window, hoping they wouldn't pick on me.

"Hey, Jessie!"

Sigh, no such luck there I guess. I ignored them and continued to stare outside, watching the landscape zip past me. I heard them snickering and several of the kids in front turned around to stare in my direction.

Out of the corner of my eye, I could see them banding together, whispering and pointing at me. I closed my eyes, wishing that the bus would just fly home instead of me having to endure this ridiculous charade.

Their snickers grew louder and I felt a warm sensation under my leg. I shrugged it off thinking that it was from the heater beneath the seat or my mind playing tricks on me. Suddenly my pants felt too hot and I looked down to see one of the guys holding a lighter beneath my leg. I jumped up, cursing at them, which made them laugh harder. Apparently one of them slid underneath the seat and flicked on the lighter while the other guys leaned in my direction to shield their antics from the front.

I looked up, checking to see if the bus driver saw their actions and sighed, dismayed that there wasn't even a flicker of awareness of what was happening back here. The driver remained completely focused on the road with barely a glance toward us. *Gee, thanks for coming to my rescue...jerk!* Hot rage rushed through my body and made my hands shake.

Not willing to put up with this crap any longer, I immediately got up and moved closer to the front in a newly vacant spot as the bus driver pierced me with a murderous glare for walking around. I glared back at the driver as I sat down with an angry huff.

I desperately wanted to read Randy's letter but I didn't dare take it out of my backpack for fear that it would be ripped to shreds by the guys on the bus. They would do anything to make me miserable and I really didn't want to give them that temptation.

The memory of Sandy's reaction to the photo of Randy was priceless and I smiled, savoring it.

Happy to be home, I admired the long blue shadows cast in the snow from the trees that lined the lane. The snow sparkled like tiny gems, reflecting every color of the rainbow like tiny gems.

Halfway down the lane, I spotted fresh deer tracks, crisscrossing the field. Its meandering path led toward the woods near the spot where I often go for my walks. I stared in that direction for a minute and suddenly noticed some movement.

At first I thought it was a patch of snow falling from the branches and waited patiently just to be sure.

Something definitely was hiding behind the trees, within the thick branches and deep snow. It strolled casually back into the field and I stood frozen, not believing my eyes. *No way*! I once again felt very lucky.

I had never seen an albino deer before and there one was, standing in my backyard along my trail. I brought my hand to my heart, in awe, thrilled to be so fortunate as to witness such a miracle. Unfortunately, it caught the movement of my hands, startled and pranced back into the forest.

Elation filled me with warmth and I instantly felt loved at the moment, thankful for the experience. *If only I had a camera*, I mused.

It was like a sign, an omen and I felt more at ease with the sense of hope in my heart. Walking back toward the house, I looked up and spotted Parker in my bedroom window, watching me.

After dumping my boots at the door and hanging up my coat, I strolled into the kitchen, made myself a cup of hot chocolate, and grabbed some ginger snaps while I checked the mail, rifling through the envelopes.

I carried my backpack and red mug up to my room and settled into my desk. Parker greeted me with a loud "purrup!" as I walked past him. He jumped up onto the desk, leaning into my face with his warm fur.

I petted him while waiting for the laptop to start up. Taking cautious sips of the hot chocolate, with steam curling upward and warming my face, I pulled out Randy's letter and read it thoroughly.

Hi! My name is Randy and I go to White Oaks High School in Calgary. I enjoy sports, particularly football and I'm currently the captain of our team this year. I love to read and watch movies. I'm a big fan of "Supernatural" and, like everyone else on this planet, Harry Potter, and the Hunger Games. By the way, aren't the Winchester brothers awesome? They're supernaturally hot!

As my eyes roamed over his words, I nearly choked on my hot chocolate at his comment about the supernaturally hot brothers, not expecting it at all. While mopping up the spots of liquid from the desk with my sleeve, I quickly finished reading the rest of his letter, noticing that he was keeping it polite and straightforward.

I wondered what to say in response as I clicked on "Mail" and selected a new draft. The blank page stared at me, waiting for the letters to dance across the screen. The cursor stubbornly blinked, waiting impatiently for its next prompt as I gathered my thoughts, trying to decide if I should keep it simple or sound clever.

Dear Randy. I began to type and then immediately deleted *Dear* and replaced it with the less personal, *Hi Randy.* I decided for to go for the honest route for now. *Nice to hear from you. Wow, Captain of the football team, that's great! You must enjoy it! I play a variety of sports, too. At the moment I'm involved with Basketball and Karate. I love to read books as well. I'll definitely check out Supernatural when I get the chance. It sounds interesting!*

I had considered revealing my hearing impairment at that point and decided not to push my luck. I didn't want to scare him away. I continued plugging away, mostly describing how small my town was. *I live in a rural community, surrounded by farmland as far as the eye can see. It's beautiful in the fall when the sunflowers are in bloom. They fill entire fields with them. How about you? Do you live in the city or country? Do you have a favorite season?*

I nibbled on the addictive ginger snaps as I came up with a few questions, trying not be intrusive and wondered if I should ask him if was seeing anyone. Ridiculous, I thought. A long distance relationship would be out of the question. My mind batted back and forth between conflicting thoughts. Yeah, but a girl can dream—who knew what could happen?

I sat back from the laptop for a moment while I debated what to say, sipping the rest of my hot chocolate before it got cold.

What do you do in spare time? Hang out with your friends? Looking forward to hearing from you soon! Sincerely, Jessie.

I quickly scanned my message for spelling mistakes before I clicked on "Send" and closed "Mail."

A message popped up from MSN stating that someone wanted permission to join my contact list. Intrigued, I said yes and was surprised to see who it was: Sandy.

Groaning, I reluctantly turned on my chat box. Her message was rather perky, drawing suspicion from me. *Hi Jessie! Wanna chat?*

I responded with a short reply. *Sure.*

She replied back instantly, like a tiger pouncing on its prey. *Great! Write to your pen pal yet?*

Aha, now we get to it, I'd wondered when she would bring that up. *Yes,* I said, not revealing anything.

Her response was short but to the point. *And?*

I kept it equally as short. *He's nice.*

She said, *Cool!* sounding a bit too polite for her style.

I was waiting for the other shoe to drop.

I asked her the same question. *What's yours like?*

She sounded disappointed. *Okay, a tad boring.*

Interesting, I thought. She was being honest here which was a stretch for her.

Danny's here, he wants to chat with you. And there it was, the sound of the other shoe dropping. I knew she was leading up to something.

Okay, chat away.

Hi Jessie. Danny here.

I had no idea what he wanted but I had this nagging suspicion in the back of my head. *Hi Danny,* I responded politely.

Doing anything tonight?

I sighed, that was the second time today they asked me that.

Homework, I typed quickly, hoping to get this over with.

Oh. Want to come over here?

I was becoming alarmed.

Why? I asked.

I like you. You're a nice girl.

Okay, this was getting creepy.

How? I can't drive and I live too far way.

No problem. I'll send a Limo.

My eyes bugged out. What? I thought, stunned by his remark. I didn't care for his attitude and I especially didn't care if he was rich. He was practically rolling in it and flaunting it now. Which turned me off big time. I was becoming more disgusted by the minute.

No thanks. I appreciate it though.

Even that didn't deter him. He continued on with a litany of juvenile prompts, sounding like a spoiled brat. *Oh come on. It'll be fun.*

Which sounded immensely fake to me. There was an undercurrent of malice in his behavior as if this was part of a dare from his friends.

I could easily imagine his sister standing beside him, telling him what to say, and snickering at my responses.

Don't you like me? he asked.

I felt like banging my head against the table. He was virtually clueless. While I was coming up with a reply, he sent another note. *Don't hurt my feelings.*

I shook my head, flabbergasted by his comments. *I would never do that to you.*

Instantly, he responded, *Thanks. That's nice of you.* He added another one without giving me a chance to say anything. *Please? Will you go out with me?*

Wow, he was desperate, which scared the crap out of me, and I had a bad feeling about this. I wasn't keen on being the laughing stock of the entire school because of his spiteful prank. After my disastrous birthday party, I had pretty much stopped trusting anyone at school.

Trying to be courteous, I said, *Sorry, I'm busy tonight. Thanks for asking.*

All he said was a curt, *Bye,* and I wondered if I really did hurt his feelings. I felt torn. I couldn't tell if he was speaking the truth or trying to make me the butt of a gigantic joke. It was becoming hard to see the truth through the lies and deceit.

Still it bothered me that I may have been too harsh with him. It was breaking my heart, and I felt deeply conflicted. Had I read the signs wrong? I wondered.

All of this second guessing was ripping me to shreds. I couldn't stand the thought of hurting someone else.

I sat at my desk, looking out the window, watching the shadows stretch across the snow, turning a vibrant shade of blue as the sun sank deeper into the sky.

Feeling scattered, I disconnected from the internet and shut the laptop. I was so flustered that I couldn't calm down and stomped downstairs for supper.

CHAPTER 7

Breaking Point

Everyone was taking their time settling in to class this morning, moving sluggishly and yawning, not wanting it to begin. There was a group of students near the back wall, chattering excitedly amongst themselves. A paper airplane floated aimlessly around the room.

Oh Goody, I thought dryly. *It must be Friday.* Not that there was anything wrong with Fridays in general, but this particular one poked at my raw nerves like someone tightening the guitar strings a smidgen too far, straining almost to the breaking point.

I was exhausted from tossing and turning all night, not sleeping a wink. My mind was in constant turmoil, taunting me endlessly.

There was no sign of Sandy or Danny as I scanned the room, feeling relieved that I didn't have to face them yet. Soon after that thought crossed my mind, they appeared in the doorway, Sandy engrossed in an animated conversation with her sidekick Barbie look-a-like and Danny holding his books tightly to his chest, head hung downwards.

I felt a twinge of guilt at the sight of his rejected body language, and I was mentally kicking myself for not being nicer to him during our last chat. I could almost hear the guitar strings quivering in my mind, straining even harder. It was literally a struggle to maintain my sanity at this point.

Crap, I thought as I watched him slink to his chair. *Crappity, crap, crap!* My tortured mind was going into overdrive. He didn't make any eye contact with anyone. He simply sat there staring at his notebooks, doodling on the cover of his binder with a black pen.

Did I really make him that miserable or is it all an act?

Dean popped into my line of vision, bouncing on his feet and full of energy. He was full of pep this morning, more hyperactive than usual. I liked Dean and his buoyant personality. He always made me smile or laugh with his dramatic flair for being the class clown. He was a natural at cracking jokes and making people laugh. He had that uncanny knack for bringing out the humor in virtually any situation. I enjoyed his presence in any class. His happy go lucky attitude was simply contagious and I loved it.

In a way, I envied him. He seemed so courageous and so bold, not caring what anyone else said about him. *He's so free.*

"Here, Jessie. This is for you." Dean handed me a bright green paper airplane that he made. Written on it was, *Fly me.*

I laughed, feeling a bit childish. "Thanks Dean."

He smiled impishly, eyes twinkling mischievously. He had such a good heart and sweet soul.

I considered giving it to Danny to cheer him up but as I was about to walk toward him, Mr. Wilson barged in carrying a pile books with a thick stack of paper on top.

When he arrived, the class grew silent and everyone scampered back to their seats, scraping loudly on the floor, like ants scampering to hide from the giant foot that was ready to stomp down on them.

I had no choice but to approach the scowling Mr. Wilson and hand over the microphone. I flicked the switch to the ON position and quickly slithered back to my desk beside Stephanie.

Mr. Wilson was known for his quick temper and stern attitude. He ran a tight ship and was strictly "all business, all the time." Come to think of it, I hadn't ever seen him smile. Today he wore black corduroy pants with a light dove-gray striped shirt and midnight black tie, which clearly reflected his dark mood.

He quickly looped the microphone over his head, grabbed a notepad from the towering pile on his desk, and strode briskly to the blackboard, snagging a piece of chalk in the process. He began to tap the chalk across the blackboard, posting one row of symbols and another row of chemical names from the periodic chart, speaking at the same time which irritated me since I couldn't lip read.

I often had to remind the teachers not to turn their backs on me when speaking since I couldn't lip-read what they were saying if I couldn't see their faces. Either he forgot or he simply didn't care today, so I put my hand up in the air, waiting for him to notice.

Meanwhile, Dean and his partner Cameron were tossing one last paper airplane off to my left, whispering loudly with snuffling laughter behind their hands.

I saw Mr. Wilson turn around, one eyebrow raised. "Dean and Cameron, anything you wish to share with us?"

The two of them went abruptly silent, uttering, "No sir," in unison.

He spotted my raised hand, sighed deeply, barely controlling the frustration displayed on his face. "Yes, Jessie?" His voice nearly dripped with disdain.

I held onto my resolve. "Mr. Wilson, I missed what you said a minute ago when you were writing on the blackboard." I could see him breathing through his nose, almost as if he was silently counting to ten.

"Sorry. As I was saying, your task is to match the symbols to their respective names which are displayed here."

I nodded at him, acknowledging his response.

He continued writing the list in silence, then turned around to face the class. "Okay class, I want everyone to work with your partners, pairing the symbols you see here. You have fifteen minutes—go."

It was a fairly straightforward exercise, some of the pairs were relatively easy, others a little bit more challenging and I liked it.

Out of the corner of my eye, I saw Cameron and Dean muttering to each other a bit loudly and breaking into fits of giggles, prompting glares from some of the students around them. Mr. Wilson glowered at them over the pile of papers on his desk.

After the fifteen minutes passed, Mr. Wilson stood, scraping his chair on the floor. He walked back to the blackboard, erased the symbols and replaced them with new list. "Okay folks, here is another set for you to solve."

By that point, Dean and Cameron's voice rose a little too high for his patience level. He glared at them. "All right you two, knock it off."

"Did you hear that? Knock it off!" said Dean, smirking.

"You knock it off first," replied Cameron.

Suddenly, Mr. Wilson was standing behind them. "Do I need to knock some sense into you two?" he roared at them furiously, slamming their heads together.

Son of a...I thought as I watched in shock. The class stared at him, stunned and abruptly silent. Both Dean and Cameron were rubbing their sides of their heads, casting their eyes downwards, solemn for the first time. My heart nearly broke at the sight of Dean, his spirit darkened, his bright soul seemingly shattered.

The class continued on, quickly and quietly, working through all of the problems. Everyone was afraid to utter a word. The room felt ominous and heavy. The stench of fear floated about our heads.

Many of us were still deeply shocked by Mr. Wilson's outburst. It had been so violent, unexpected, and wrong.

I glanced at Dean from time to time, hoping that his spirit would lift just a little bit. No one deserved to be treated in that manner, regardless of their actions. Dean, most of all, was the least likely person to have earned this form of punishment.

Finally, the class bell rang and virtually every student made a beeline for the door, eager to get out as quickly as possible. I had no choice but to approach Mr. Wilson to get the microphone. He slapped it down into my hand without an ounce of consideration.

I spun around and dashed out after Dean, hoping to restore his spirit. I called after him, "Dean! Wait!" I saw him slow down momentarily and I took that opportunity to catch up to him.

"Dean, I'm so sorry. He had no right to treat you like that." I looked at him, his face devoid of any of the emotion I'd seen earlier today. He looked utterly dejected, miserable from head to toe.

He mumbled, "S'allright."

Shocked I said, "No! It's not all right. You should report this to the principal!" I tried to look into his eyes but I couldn't see them for his gaze was glued to the floor. "Would you please a least consider it? Just think about it? I'll back you up."

He nodded slowly, still deeply affected by Mr. Wilson's actions with no trace of his former bubbly personality.

An idea popped into my head that just might work. "Dean, I'm going to an audition sometime in the next few weeks. Will you come with me? I think you would be a great addition to the cast."

I saw a flicker of light in his eyes as he thought about it, so I continued my pleas. "You would be a natural! It's perfect!"

Finally, he spoke up. "Sure. Yeah. Maybe that would work."

I watched him walk way, biting my lip, worried about him. I had never seen this side of him, so dark and withdrawn.

Tiffany and Brooklyn appeared by my side, chattering non-stop about the latest movie they had watched, filling their dialogue with ridiculously superficial remarks. "...like...wow...that dress she wore...so cool." Which left me wondering how they managed to get through school with so much air in their heads.

They embodied the classic definition of spoiled brats with money to burn, flaunting it through their use of glossy makeup and outfits so flashy they would make a Nun pass out in shock. Those two set my teeth on edge with their perpetually perky chatter whenever they were within a few feet within of me.

A mental image of me ripping out a Chanel ad from a fashion magazine and stapling it to their foreheads made me feel instantly better.

All three of us were heading in the same direction whether I liked it or not. My mood was getting more sour by the minute.

Tiffany took a moment from her ongoing chatter to inhale and noticed me for the first time. "Oh hey, Jessie! Say—did you hear what happened in Mr. Wilson's class?"

"Yes, I was there," I replied, glowering at her, trying to discourage her from going any further.

"Oh." She said as her face fell, disappointed that she could not be the queen of gossip.

Brooklyn chimed in, "So, is it true that he really did that to Dean and Cameron?"

Oh my God, could they get any more vapid? I thought darkly.

"It was cruel and completely uncalled for. He had no right to hurt them like that. Mr. Wilson should be fired for his actions," I spat out, angry at their lack of comprehension. I picked up the pace and was relieved once I stepped into Mr. Makena's class.

He was sitting on the edge of his desk, smiling broadly, his dark chocolate skin glowing. He wore a vibrant orange shirt, opened at the collar, with a tan jacket and pants, and dark brown suede shoes. His eyes twinkled with pure joy, happy to be around the students. He clearly loved his role as a teacher.

I always enjoyed his history lessons. He managed to bring the most interesting and, at times, the most disgusting stories to life. His passion was simply contagious. He loved sharing it with us, practically acting out the scenes in front of us.

I crossed over to his desk, handing the equipment over to him.

He accepted it with a smile. "Thanks, Jessie."

He was one of the few teachers in school who understood my hearing impairment and consciously arranged his teaching style to make everything easier for me. He rarely turned his back to the class when he spoke and was aware of the difficulties caused by him pacing back and forth since I would likely get dizzy trying to follow his lips.

He also knew not to stand in front of the windows, knowing that his face would be hidden in the shadows.

As I sat down, Mr. Makena went back to fiddling with his laptop, plugging in the wires for the projector. Once he was finished, he strode over the wall and flicked off the lights, yanking down the white viewing screen.

"All right settle down, guys. Today I have decided to do something a little different," he said as a murmur ran through the class.

"As many of you already know, I'm originally from Africa. Botswana to be more specific.

"I came to Canada to become a teacher. Unfortunately this meant leaving my village and my family." The screen brightened before our eyes, displaying a scene of a dry, barren land with sandy hills in the background. There were very few trees, mostly prickly bushes that dotted the landscape. A jeep stood parked in the center of the screen with Mr. Makena leaning against it.

It took me a few moments to recognize him. He was so thin and young in the image, dressed simply, wearing a T-shirt and cargo pants with sandals. It was a stark contrast to what he wore today.

He continued, describing the wildlife, average temperatures, and rainfall, changing the slides to show animals along the road. Zebras ran wild in the sparse fields along with the elephants and giraffes in the distance.

It was such a shock to see these slides, realizing that they were real and not from some documentary on television. This was a true connection to his life in another country, opening my eyes to a very different way of life.

I leaned on my desk, listening to his story of growing up in Africa, a place so far away from us, so unbelievably disconnected from our lives that it seemed surreal. I simply could not grasp the vast differences between our lifestyles. They were worlds apart.

Logan raised his hand, curiously asking if it ever snowed in Africa. The class roared with laughter, prompting his face to flush a shade of beet red.

Mr. Makena raised his hands to calm the class. "Actually, Logan, that was a valid question. Yes, it can snow in Africa. Particularly places in South Africa, such as Uganda, and at high altitudes like Mt. Kilimanjaro." The class was in awe, silenced by his response. "It's rare but it does happen."

He proceeded to the next slide, which depicted several teenagers, two girls and three boys, standing together in a group, all smiles. "Ah," he remarked. "This is one of my favorite pictures." He smiled as he gazed toward the screen.

"These are my younger sisters and cousins. They are about the same age as you."

They stood beside a simple brick building, plain in its design, a nearby tree providing shade for them. "This is their school which was built by hand with virtually everyone in the village helping out with the construction. They try their best to attend classes regularly, but it's not easy because there are no school buses and they live in fear of being attacked by the local rebels."

The next slide showed a sparse room with a few simple tables and chairs, part of the wall crumbling. There were no cheery posters anywhere, no books or other items that were commonly seen here at school. Upon observing this image, I felt humbled.

Mr. Makena revealed how difficult it was for them to obtain books and school supplies, such as papers and pens, objects that were readily available to us. He also indicated that medicine was scarce and that they were prone to suffer illnesses that didn't exist here.

I felt very fortunate to have the luxury of a warm home, clothes, my laptop—even if it was second hand—and hearing aids. Even though my hearing aids set back my parents several thousand dollars, I simply could not imagine anyone in Africa even being able to even afford the batteries for them. Here the batteries would last an average of two weeks before they sputtered and died. Then all I had to do was open the blistered package and replace them with new ones. It would be virtually impossible in Africa to do the same thing as easily as I did here.

My mind reeled at how much we took for granted. I was absorbing those thoughts as the bell rang and I continued thinking about them for the rest of the day. My mind swirled with nonstop images of Africa, more personal now that I knew someone who came from there as opposed to viewing a photo in the newspaper.

I mused about it on my trip back home, completely ignoring everyone on the bus, deep in thought.

My thoughts switched over to Dean as I put my backpack down on the floor in my room and spotted the airplane he made earlier. I picked it up and tossed it around my room. Parker danced on the floor, reaching for it with his paws, bringing a smile to my face once again.

CHAPTER 8

Pen Pal

My fingers danced across the keyboard as I typed a reply to Randy's latest message. It had been a while since I had written a pen pal letter to him and, as always, I struggled to come up some interesting conversation.

We had talked briefly about our favorite books, top songs, bits and pieces of our lives, compared our schools and of course, sports. I was blown away by his success in sports, particularly football. He'd previously revealed that he was the star of his team, which made me wonder if he was overdoing it in terms of gloating.

I'd told him about the pranks that some of my classmates had played on me and he responded that they were just being stupid. I agreed but it still hurt.

Hi Randy. It's good to hear from you again. How's life treating you these days? I typed briskly, trying to sound casual and interested. Our pen pal relationship was not growing any closer since we didn't have much of a connection. We'd already shared our thoughts on some our favorite topics and it was becoming more of a challenge to keep the conversations fresh, particularly since some of his responses were somewhat curt.

I had gotten the impression that he was only being polite simply because he was required to do this assignment.

The keys clicked softly as I shared my thoughts. *Oh hey! Did you know that Kurt from Glee is on Twitter? Isn't that awesome? I loved his joke about baseball. He told his Dad that he had perfect pitch but he wasn't impressed. Get it? Music pitch versus baseball pitch...Ha!*

The cursor blinked at I sat there wondering what else to add. We had traded several quips about the weather and school closures. I hadn't told him about my hearing impairment and was still hesitant to reveal that to him. I wanted to keep this as normal possible and in some ways still private, separate from school.

Despite my complaints about my classmates, he did not offer any clue that he suspected the true reason behind it. I was not ready to tell him.

I added a few more sentences about the success of some of the sports teams around here but came up blank again.

"How about this?" I muttered as I typed. *I'm a big scifi geek and adore shows like Warehouse 13. I also love Fringe, it's so weird and totally out there. Although it grosses me out sometimes, too.* I gingerly added that last fact knowing that he would probably cringe upon reading it, but I wanted to keep our conversation engaged.

I also added a few notes that I had been taking self-defense and enjoying it.

I clicked on "Send" and went back to my homework, finishing up the essay for Mrs. Evans, methodically checking it for spelling mistakes since she was a stickler for details like that.

An hour later, Randy sent back a reply, the fastest one yet. Impressive, I thought. He usually doesn't respond until days later.

I clicked on his message, prompting it to open and read it eagerly, my eyes stopping at his response about the shows. Stunned I went back and read it again.

Oh yeah! He totally rocks! I love Glee too! Hey, can you send me his Twitter handle? It would be so cool to follow him!

I narrowed my eyes suspiciously at that remark. Huh? I pondered that for a while, trying to make sense of it. *Could he be...nah...*

I didn't know what to say to him at the moment. I was still speechless and closed it to focus on my homework, which was due tomorrow.

It was late when I went to bed, and I struggled to sleep, tossing and turning throughout the night. I woke up feeling edgy, having not slept much. My body felt exhausted.

It wasn't until the lunch hour that I snapped back to reality when Sandy approached me in the cafeteria. I had seen her reading messages on her cell phone in between classes, noticing her glance over her shoulder at me from time to time.

She stood in front of me wearing a long indigo blue sweater with a light cornflower blue shirt, crisp pleated jeans, and—wait for it—midnight blue cowboy boots. Her hands were fisted on her hips with her fingers drumming out an irritated, staccato rhythm. Her face was flushed with anger. I looked up at her after pulling an apple from my lunch bag and taking a bite out of it as she impatiently tapped her toe on the floor.

"What?" I asked in between bites, my voice somewhat muffled.

She snorted at me in disgust. "You know what!" she snarled, spitting the last word out forcefully.

"Uh. No, I don't." *What in the world was she talking about?* I thought back to this morning trying to recall if I'd said anything to her friends.

"This! This is what I'm talking about!" She thrust the phone in my face, displaying a texted message. I stared at it for a moment, utterly confused until I saw who it was from.

I burst out laughing, pounding the table with my fist, tears started to run out of the corners of my eyes. Now it all made sense.

Sandy had gone behind my back—no surprise there—and had gotten Randy's email address. At this point, I didn't care what she'd done. His answer was a sweet revenge to her actions.

She thrust it into my face again, his words, *I'm gay,* clearly displayed, and I started laughing again and spluttering. "I didn't know!" I said between wheezing laughs. "Honestly!"

"Liar! You did this on purpose!" she said. Still angry, she turned on her heels and stormed away, her troop of Barbie look-a-likes tagging along.

I stared after her as everything started to fall into place, the missing pieces in Randy's messages now made sense. There were times when he had been cryptic, somewhat vague when I asked about his personal life. And finally, the recent revelation about his favorite show.

I smiled, savoring the moment, her look of abject horror when she tried to use her feminine wiles on him, not realizing it was a wasted effort.

At least it explained some of the distance between us. There was no personal connection. Even though a part of me was stung by her backhanded tactics, the end result was totally worth it.

As I walked back to my locker, I had a feeling that I wouldn't be hearing from him anytime soon.

At least I had tonight's class at the dojo to look forward to, I mused, excited at the prospect of getting my uniform and belt.

My eyes glazed over for most of the subjects in the afternoon classes, finding them a bit dull.

I quickly went through my homework as soon as I got home, and wolfed down my supper, anxious to go to karate.

Mom dropped me off at the dojo on her way to do some grocery shopping. She stopped in front of the brightly lit building with its large glass windows on either side of the entrance, its walls lined with trophies.

She waved at me before driving away. "Bye! Have fun!" I rolled my eyes at her and gave her a reluctant wave in return.

I slung my gym bag over my shoulder, pulled open the door, stopping to take off my boots and place them on the mats beneath the sign displaying "Please remove footwear before entering the dojo – thanks."

I looked around wondering where to go next, my eyes roaming around past the large display of equipment for sale, warm up suits, and various merchandise with the karate logo splayed across them. I stared at the impressive wall filled with trophies, some of which were taller than me.

"Jessie! It's great to see you here!" As he strolled toward me, Ethan's voice boomed across the lobby, prompting a few parents to look in our direction. He reached out and shook my hand politely. "Excited yet?"

I gulped. "Somewhat, believe it or not. A bit nervous too."

He smiled. "Ah, that's okay. You'll get used to this fairly soon."

My heart skipped a few beats and I had to stifle a sigh of contentment, mentally restraining myself.

I dimly realized I was still holding onto his hand. I looked down in alarm. "Oh sorry! Guess you want that hand back, eh?"

He winked at me, making my insides melt. "Don't worry about it. All righty then. Let's see, you'll need a uniform and belt...probably size 2 or 3..." he muttered as he went into the office, rifling through the shelves of neatly stacked uniforms and pulled out the one he wanted. He grabbed a white belt and placed it on top of the pile in his arms.

His smile broadened as he turned around and marched in my direction. He transferred the pile of clothing into my arms. "Here we are. You're all set to go. Now before you get changed, here's a tip. There are small thin pieces of fabric on either side of the uniform, the trick is to cross the flap across your body and tie it to the thin strips, okay?" He looked into my eyes as he finished his instructions, and I gulped again, breathing to clear my head.

He pointed toward a door off to my right. "There's the ladies' locker room. Oh! Regarding your belt, I'll help you with that when you come back out."

I nodded. "Sure. Over there?" I gestured with my head in the general direction he'd indicated. He nodded back.

Balancing the uniform in my arms, I walked over to the locker room, and pushed the door open with my shoulder. There were already several students in the room, some fully dressed in their crisp white uniforms. Two of them wore a white belt, one a yellow, and the other one had an orange belt.

They looked to be about my age, one maybe a little older. They glanced up from tying their belts as I entered the room. I found a spot on the bench and took off my jeans and pullover, wondering if I should wear a T-shirt underneath my uniform. As if reading my mind, one of the students suggested I wear one. "Believe me. Your uniform will become loose during class. You'll want something under it as a precaution."

I smiled shyly at her. "Oh, thanks for the tip."

I pulled on the pants, tightening the drawstring and attempted to put on the top part of the uniform rather unsuccessfully. It was trickier than it looked.

The older student stepped forward. "Here, let me help you with that." She showed me how to tie it off at the sides then looked up, smiling. "Is this your first class here?"

"Um. Yes and no. I took self-defense classes at school before coming here. This is my first time here though."

"That's great! I'm Molly by the way."

"I'm Jessie." I reached out and shook her hand.

"Oops, gotta go. Don't forget to take off your jewelry," she remarked as she exited the room with rest of the group.

"Thanks!" I said over my shoulder.

I reached up to my ears, removed my hoop earrings, and unlatched my watch from my wrist.

I picked up my belt, wondering what was the correct way of putting it on. I sighed, frustrated and decided to ask Ethan who was probably waiting for me.

Sure enough, he was standing in the lobby talking to another instructor who wore a black belt, his sleeves covered in various badges.

They were both similar in their age and appearance, equally as tall and fit. Ethan's friend's hair was raven black and rather spiky, the ends pointing in all directions.

The two of them looked at me as I approached Ethan. Spiky-haired dude took the cue to disappear. "I'll see you in class." They did a knuckle bump as they went their separate ways.

Curious, I glanced toward the other instructor. "That's Sensei Jake. Don't worry, you'll like him, he's a nice guy." He looked down at my hands still holding the white belt.

"I'll help you with that." He grabbed it from my hand, walked behind me, and proceeded to wrap it around my waist. "Watch how I do this."

I found it unnervingly distracting to have his arms around me. He tucked one end up underneath the belt and pulled the two ends together into a tight knot. "You'll notice that there is a difference in the way our belts are tied, particularly for in-between ranks." He pointed at his belt. "Black belts do not cross the obi at the back."

He turned around to demonstrate and I tried hard not to gaze at his butt for too long. "And you will also see different uniforms. The instructors wear black pants and white tops, which are called Gi's."

I recalled the badges on Sensei Jake's uniform and noticed that Ethan had some of them on his sleeve as well. I ran my fingers over his badges. "What are these for?"

He glanced down at his arm, pointing at each one. "This one is for being on the Demo team, this one is weapons training, and this one is for the sparring team."

He continued. "Some of us are on teams. We do different things such as going to tournaments or doing demonstrations at events like the mall or schools. It's a mark of our achievements."

He looked toward the class and gently guided me through the door. "We always bow as we enter the dojo, and when we leave, always facing toward the mirrors to show respect." He snapped his feet together and clapped the sides of legs with his hands, bowing at the waist. He turned to me. "Go ahead and try it."

I nervously stepped just past the doorframe, put my feet together with my arms at my sides and bowed. The floor felt cool beneath my feet as I walked in.

Ethan smiled eagerly. "Perfect! Let's line up with the rest of the class." He steered me toward the end of the line of students facing the mirrors that stretched from wall to wall, ceiling to floor. "Lower belts line up at this end, higher belts line up at the other end."

He left my side, walked briskly to the front of the class, and stood beside Sensei Jake.

Ethan barked out the commands as he began the class. "Keske!" "Rei!"

We all bowed in unison.

"Before we start our warm up, I wanted to announce that we have a new student with us today and her name is Jessie." He smiled as he gestured toward me with an open hand.

"So, let's make her feel welcome." He started to applaud prompting the rest of the class to join in.

I felt slightly embarrassed at the attention, feeling my face go red. I muttered a shy thank you to them and did a slight wave with my hand.

Both Ethan and Jake led the group in a clockwise direction, running around the room, forward and backward, changing directions randomly. Then we switched to push ups, sit ups, and strenuous leg stretches that I thought would never end. We all stood in a circle practicing a variety of stances as we worked on our high blocks and low blocks while the instructors delivered strikes at us with a giant padded bat.

Then we practiced punches and back-fist strikes. After the warm up and basic drills, we were divided into small groups according to our belt levels and shown how to do a kata, which reminded me of a waltz. We stepped forward to block, then moved to another angle to strike, pivoted around to deliver another block, and followed up with a punch.

The stances were very specific, flowing from place to another like a gentle dance, yet each carried an undertone of power. Our strikes at the end of each sequence were to be delivered accurately with force and determination. It was a demanding workout since my mind and body was not yet accustomed to such unusual motions and focus.

During the last fifteen minutes of class, a sparring session was held for those who wanted to work on their fighting skills.

We sat down, with our legs crossed and hands on our knees, on the outside of the ring. It was actually a large square of red tape on the floor. Four of the students picked up their gym bags from the wall and began strapping on their shin pads, gloves, helmets, and mouth guards. The helmets looked soft and were covered with vents.

Ready for action, two of the students stood beside the line, hands out in front, in a rigid stance. The other two knelt down with their legs tucked underneath.

Sensei Ethan stood in the center of the ring and gave them permission to enter. The two students bowed, prior to stepping into the ring, and took their places, facing each other in the center.

"Bow to me," Sensei Ethan said, facing both of them. "Then face each other and bow. Now, go into your fighting stance."

As they took a step back with one foot, arms raised, he placed his hand in between them like a barrier.

"Ready?" He looked at both of them as they nodded, then declared, "Hajime!" as he took away his hand.

The two of them stared at each other for moment, gauging their opponent.

The yellow belt delivered a fast sidekick, which was slapped away by the orange belt. Their ponytails bounced as they danced around each other.

The orange belt swung around with two rapid kicks, the first one to the ribs, the other near the head. There was no impact at all since the kick stopped short, a few inches away.

I was impressed by the amount of control they displayed. I could sense their eagerness as they tested each other's reflexes.

Sensei Ethan interrupted the fight. "Halt!" They immediately went back to their starting positions in the center and faced each other with their arms outstretched and rigid. He gestured sharply in the direction of the orange belt. "Point! Fighting stance." He waited for them to take their positions. "Hajime!"

They danced around each other again, deliberating their next moves, like tigers waiting to pounce.

The yellow belt made the first move with a back-fist strike that was quickly blocked then followed with a punch to the ribs and a loud, "Kiai," that echoed across the room.

"Halt!" Once again, they went back to their posts as Sensei Ethan gave out another point to the orange belt. They went at each other again, the tension even thicker now, throwing the odd kick and punch which went on for a minute or two.

At the end, Sensei Ethan raised his arm toward the orange belt declaring her the winner.

The next two participants stood up as the exhausted competitors bowed and sat down, wiping sweat from their faces and taking off their helmets.

I sat rooted to the spot, slack jawed and impressed by their competitive nature.

I continued to watch the next fight, eagerly analyzing their moves, learning how they sized each other up. It wasn't easy to keep track since they moved so quickly and efficiently.

Once the bout was over, they took off their equipment, stuffed it back into their bags, and placed them along the wall, chatting amicably to each other in good spirits. We all lined up at the front of the class facing the mirrors, adjusting our uniforms here and there.

Sensei Ethan and Sensei Jake stood before us, eyes roaming the rows.

"Before we bow out, we will spend the next few minutes meditating. I would like everyone to go into a kneeling position with their hands on their knees please," requested Sensei Ethan calmly.

Everyone went down smoothly, one leg then the other, tucking them underneath, sitting as still as statues.

"Remember to breathe in and out deeply as you release the tension from your body. Zazen." He spoke softly but firmly. "And clear your mind. Mokuso."

It was eerily quiet throughout the dojo except for the deep breaths around me. After a few minutes of meditation, there was a loud clap. "Open your eyes. Stand up please so that we may bow out.

"Keske!" All of us snapped to attention, slapping the sides of our legs. "Rei!"

Following along, we bowed toward the instructors.

"Arigato," Sensei Ethan added just before we were dismissed.

I looked at him with a puzzled expression and asked him, "Arigato? What does it mean?"

Amused he replied, "It means thank you."

"Oh, cool."

"So what did you think of your first class?" he asked casually as we strolled out of the classroom.

"I was impressed. The sparring was awesome. What did you call it?" I asked, fiddling nervously with my belt.

He smiled. "It's Kumite."

"Wow, there's so many words to learn..." I trailed off trying to remember them.

His eyes lit up. "Hang on a sec—I'll give you a sheet with the terminology."

He walked over to the office, went through a stack of papers, and picked up a bunch of sheets stapled together. "Here you go. I guess you could call that your homework for tonight. There is all sorts of interesting information in there, including the origin of Martial Arts, our student creed, rules, and our schedule." He flipped through them quickly, pointing out the pages he'd mentioned, and added, "And my email address is on the bottom of the schedule should you have any questions."

"Would you like my email address?" I asked. "Just in case I make a mistake and can't get through."

"Sure that would be great." He grabbed a pen off the desk from the office, practically skipping back to me. I scribbled it down, checking to make sure it was legible before giving it back to him.

"Great! I'll be in touch!"

I walked backward to the locker room, did a half wave, then pivoted around and narrowly missed colliding with Molly as she stepped out of the door.

"Oh! Excuse me!" I muttered, hoping against hope, he hadn't witnessed my clumsiness.

Mom was already in the parking lot, finished with her chores, as I pranced to the car and slid in.

CHAPTER 9

Sanctuary

It had gotten much colder in the past few weeks, and the snow was getting deeper. I shivered as thick snowflakes swirled around me. The sidewalk in front of me was dark. As I made my way to the mall that was another block away, my breath was visible in the cold air. The wind had picked up strength during the past two hours I had spent in the dojo. Mom had agreed to meet me at the mall since she had some errands to run tonight, and in hindsight, I regretted that decision. I pulled my jacket closer to my body trying to block out the wind.

The wind wreaked havoc with my hearing aids, blocking out every sound around me. It drove me nuts since it was irritating and uncomfortably loud. I shivered as another blast of cold air slammed into my face, forcing me to turn my head away from it.

I passed several stores that were still open, their florescent lights spilling out onto the sidewalk. At that moment, I could swear I heard a whistle or someone yelling at me. I looked up into the fierce wind, squinting my eyes, but not seeing anyone in front of me. Strange, I thought. Maybe it was my imagination. I continued on, staggering slightly from the wind.

I heard it again, this time mixed with voices that were loud but didn't make any sense. Then, I saw their shadows behind me. Gulping back the fear that was rising through my body, I picked up the pace, more afraid than ever. Suddenly, a big shove across my back sent me stumbling awkwardly. I frantically tried to regain my balance. Someone grabbed my shoulder and spun me around.

"What's the matter with you?" demanded the tall one standing in the middle of the group, his black hair spiky and facing all directions, an earring gleaming in the dull light. He sneered at me, and shoved at my shoulder roughly. "Hey! Didn't you hear us? We've been calling you from way back there." He jerked his thumb over his shoulder in the general direction of where I had been walking.

His pals stood beside him, equally menacing, holding their hockey sticks in their hands, with their large bulky bags on their shoulders. It was obvious they had come from the arena not too far from the dojo.

One of them leaned in toward me, as recognition dawned across his face. "Well, if ain't Kung Fu Barbie." He laughed rudely, looking at his pals.

He swung at my face, slapping his palm across my cheek, trying to get a reaction out of me. I instinctively brought my hands upward blocking his strikes, which made him angrier and more aggressive. I knocked his hands away, causing his heavy bag to fall to the ground with a thud, and sending his stick clattering to the sidewalk.

He bent down to retrieve it, full of rage. "Nice going, bitch!"

I tried to turn around, starting to walk backward, ready to run, when he abruptly yanked me back with the hook of his stick in the crook of my elbow.

I tried to shrug out of it, pushing it away from me when he suddenly lifted it up and roughly pulled at my neck with the blade of his stick. He yanked the stick hard, trying to pull me toward him, but I kept batting at it, trying to stop him. He reached for me again, this time, hitting my ear before I managed to absorb a portion of the blow with my arm.

I gasped from the pain and shock, reached up to clutch my now empty ear, blood running down my neck. My eyes watered, making it difficult to see as I frantically tried to search the ground for my hearing aid.

"Hey! What's your problem?" they yelled, closing in on me.

The situation was becoming dire very quickly now that I couldn't hear them. I could see them moving their lips, anger clearly etched on their faces.

I brought up my hand protectively against my pounding ear. My hands shook violently. As the tall one approached me, he grabbed my jacket and pulled me toward him. I delivered a swift kick to his groin, thankful my mind was clear enough to remember that technique.

He went down on one knee in pain, squeaking like a mouse. Grimacing, he ordered them to go after me. One of them shoved me into the chest of his pal, who pulled me into a bear hug. "What's the matter," he said in a rude sneer. "You deaf?"

"As a matter of fact she is, *jerk*."

He spun around, finding Ethan standing behind him, holding onto my gym bag. He was very angry and barely able to control it, literally vibrating with rage.

He sneered at Ethan, obviously not believing him. "Oh, come on man. You're lying."

Furious, Ethan yelled at them, "How dare you pick on her! She can't even hear you!"

I watched him in shock, wondering where he had come from as I feebly tried to follow his words.

Stunned, the guys in the group looked at each other and immediately took off in opposite directions, releasing me from their grip. Ethan reached out and grabbed the one who'd struck me earlier. "Oh, no, you don't. You're coming with me." He pulled the hockey player's jacket down to his elbows, trapping his arms, and held tightly onto the fabric.

Ethan took a step toward me, gently touching my chin as he looked at the side of my face, deeply concerned. When he saw the blood, he uttered a curse, briefly closing his eyes in anger. "Son of a...Jessie, look at me. Can you walk back to the dojo with me?" He carefully enunciated the words, making sure I could understand him.

My hands trembled, blood still seeping through my fingers. I nodded numbly at him. He reached down, grabbed my hand, and started to walk back. I winced as pain radiated down my neck and into my arm. "Wait! I can't! I have to find my hearing aid!"

I started to panic and bent down, searching the ground with my fingers, weeping.

"No, it's okay," Ethan said as he tried to pull me back up.

"Oh my God! Don't you get it? I can't afford it!"

He tugged at my hand again. "Hush, it's okay. I can help. Don't worry about it."

I looked up at him, feeling a sense of urgency. I slowly stood up, resigned, and held onto his hand for dear life as my mind tried to gather its wits through the pain.

As he burst through the doors of the dojo, Ethan called out, "Dad! I need some help here!" He guided the hockey player in front of him, while tenderly holding onto my hand. His father rushed toward us, bewildered by the chaotic scene before him. He glanced quickly at me, saw the blood on my face and hands, and immediately grabbed the teenager. Jonas forced him to sit down, standing beside him with his hand on his shoulder.

"Ethan, grab some ice and a towel for Jessie. It will help slow the bleeding and reduce the swelling." Jonas looked down at the teenager, then back up. "Go, I'll watch him while you help her."

Ethan pulled me into the office and guided me toward the couch, his face set in a worried expression. "I'll be right back," he said. Before he walked away, he brushed the hair out of my face, softly touching my cheek.

I closed my eyes, resting my head on the couch, willing the pain to go away. Within a minute, Ethan was back, holding a white towel in his hand. He touched my knee as he knelt down, looking up at me. He placed the towel in my hand and guided it to my ear, pressing lightly. I winced at the pressure.

"Sorry," he said as he saw my reaction. "I'm going to talk to Dad for a minute okay?" he said and I nodded briefly.

I watched the two of them talk to each other, both looking at me from time to time. After a minute, his father picked up the phone and spoke quickly, occasionally glancing down at the seated figure.

Ethan strode back into the office and sat down beside me. "Dad's just called the police, so they'll be here shortly." He reached up and wiped a tear from my cheek. "Here, let me hold onto this for you."

"How did you know?' I asked him.

He looked at me quizzically. "What do you mean?"

"How did you find me?"

"Oh, I was returning your bag," he explained, his face looking a bit too pale.

"Seriously? What are the chances of that happening?" I pondered on that for a moment. "It's like it was meant to happen."

"Yeah, I don't know about that. I think that I should've been there sooner," he said as he pulled me to his chest, wrapping his arms around me.

We sat there for a few minutes. The ice felt cool through the towel. Alarm raced through me as I thought about my missing hearing aid. He sensed my sudden tension and saw the worried look on my face. "Hey it's okay, we got him and the police will press charges against him."

"No, that's not it." I took a shaky breath to calm my nerves. "I don't know what to do about my hearing aid. My parents can't afford it. They are so expensive!"

"Tell you what. Why don't we let my dad talk to your parents about this? They may be able to come up with a solution." He gave me a gentle smile, apparently hoping to ease my concerns.

"This was my fault. I should have done a better job at defending myself. I feel like such an idiot!" I was deeply embarrassed that I hadn't reacted as fast I should have or used more of my strikes.

He leaned back to look directly at me, shifting his weight to the side. "Jessie, look at me. From what I saw, you did a great job. Keeping it simple works best and that's what you did. When we're scared we sometimes freeze on the spot or forget the more complicated moves. I especially like that kick you delivered."

I looked at him then dropped my eyes. "I just wish I could've done more," I said, feeling so vulnerable.

"Please don't worry about it. It takes time to develop quick reflexes. And, honestly? I'm the one who should've been there sooner," he said, as remorse filled his eyes.

The police arrived a few minutes later. They took a look at the cut on my ear and the bruises along my neck, and took couple of photographs as evidence. One of them stood beside Ethan as he recounted the events, helping me to follow their dialogue.

The policewoman took another look at my ear. "I really think you should go to the hospital to have that checked out. You might need stitches," she added, clucking over me like a mother hen. I wouldn't be surprised if she had kids herself and was used to bandaging their cuts and scrapes.

Despite her crisp uniform and thick belt filled to the brim with the tools of the trade, she gave me the impression that she was a genuinely kind person. Her brown hair was cropped in short feathery tufts with blond highlights, possibly in an attempt to appear more youthful.

I saw through the door that they were in the process of putting handcuffs on the teenager, clicking the metal shut around his wrists. He bent his head downwards, avoiding the angry stares from the onlookers as the police guided him through the door toward the cruiser.

Sensei Jonas walked up to stand beside Ethan, reaching out with his hand, and placing it on his shoulder. "I've contacted her mother and she is going to meet us at the hospital." He looked at the police officer off to my left side. "Is there anything else you need?"

She shook her head. "No sir, that's everything."

"Thank you for your help in this matter. I appreciate it," he said as he shook her hand and then turned around to speak to me. "Okay, ready to go?

He shifted his gaze to Ethan. "Can you grab her bag, her purse, and anything else she might need at the hospital?"

Ethan spun around, looked for my stuff, picked it up, and stood by the door to hold it open as I walked through. Sensei Jonas took long, quick strides to the car and opened the side door for me as Ethan turned off the lights and locked the dojo.

I climbed into the back seat, grabbed my seatbelt, and snicked it closed as Ethan slid in beside me, placing my bag on the floor. He placed his hand on my shoulder for comfort while I continued to press the towel to my sore ear.

After several minutes of zipping past streetlights and intersections, we pulled into the curved driveway in front of the Emergency Room and piled out, stepping quickly toward the triage area. The nurse took one look at me and told me to sit down. As she grabbed a clipboard, Ethan explained in detail what had happened. She nodded as she recorded the information, then took my vital signs, and jotted down my allergies onto the admit form.

She leaned forward and lifted the towel away from my ear, took a brief glance at it, and jotted more information on the form. "All right my dear, I would like you to go into that room, and one of the nurses will be with you in just a moment." She turned slightly sideways and pointed down the hallway to her right.

Ethan and I walked down the short corridor, found the indicated room, and sat down on the bed, the sheets crinkling as I shifted my weight. His father stayed behind to wait for my mother. Within minutes, a perky nurse in hot pink scrubs with a broad smile marched in, a clipboard in her hand. "Well, let's see what we have here, shall we?" she said cheerily as she took the towel out of my hand. "All righty then. Could you please lie back on the pillow?"

I took off my bulky jacket, gave it to Ethan, and settled onto the bed, feeling awkward. She rolled a small metal table to my side with green packages on top. Holding a large gauze pad in her hand, she squirted some fluid onto it from a bottle nearby. "Now hold still. I'm going to clean up your ear, okay?"

Ethan sat down on a chair beside me, leaned forward, and grasped my hand. He looked up at the nurse as she briskly dabbed the gauze on my ear. "Just to let you know, she's hard of hearing. She is missing one of her hearing aids and may not be able to hear you very well."

The nurse stood there blinking. "Oh! I'm so sorry!" she responded loudly, causing the other patients in the room to glance in my direction.

"You don't need to yell, just speak clearly and face her when you talk to her," said Ethan.

She nodded and continued to clean my ear. Satisfied, she threw the bloody gauze into a nearby trash receptacle and proceeded to open the green fabric package that was held together with tape covered in stripes.

Curious about the tape, I asked her what it was.

"Hmm? Oh, that means it sterilized," she said with a gentle grin as she set out the surgical instruments on the tray.

Just then, a slim doctor breezed in, wearing a long white lab coat, with a stethoscope around his neck. He wore green scrubs and his running shoes peeked from beneath the hem. "Hello! I'm Dr. Bartlett and you must be Jessie," he said cheerfully in a booming voice, his cheeks rosy with a healthy glow. His tousled dark brown hair was starting to turn white along the sides and a tiny earring peeked through on one earlobe. He flipped through the chart, muttering to himself, "Uh huh, I see," then walked over to the side of the bed to take a closer look at my ear. "Ah, yes. This will require a few stitches, Jessie." He looked back at my face as he spoke. "Don't panic. I will inject some freezing stuff and you won't feel a thing. Okay?"

I nodded numbly and he turned to the tray, picked up a long needle, and filled it with clear fluid from a small vial. He looked up, pulled the bright reflective lamp closer to me, and leaned in toward my ear. I could feel Ethan grip my hand tighter.

"There now, that wasn't so bad was it?" He was right. After the initial sting of the needle, my ear went totally numb. "It looks like I'll need to do about four or five stitches and that should do the trick," he said as he picked up the curved needle from the tray, leaned in, and started to sew. I could swear that I heard him humming as he worked deftly along the edge of my ear.

Out of the corner of my eye, I saw Mom and Ethan's father standing in the hallway, talking to each other. Her hand flew to her mouth in shock as he recounted tonight's events and she looked at me with wide, stunned eyes.

Ethan followed my gaze and looked over his shoulder, watching the two of them talk. Her jacket was draped across her arm and she was rifling through her purse. She handed him a business card and the two of nodded at each other in some sort of agreement.

Dr. Bartlett worked swiftly as he cut the thread and moved along to the next section. "I'm almost finished here and then you can go home." His eyes darted briefly to the door. "Is that your mom out there?"

"Yes, it is," I said quietly, wondering what she was discussing with Ethan's father.

He tilted his head in the direction of Ethan. "And who is this strapping young man sitting here?"

"This is Ethan. He's the one who stopped the scuffle tonight." I looked at Ethan and our eyes met. His face was filled with concern.

"Scuffle? I wouldn't call it a scuffle..." Ethan's words trailed off as he looked up at Dr. Bartlett.

Just then, Mom and Sensei Jonas walked in and stood beside Ethan. His father placed his hand on Ethan's shoulder and looked down at him. Mom stared at me in shock, her hands tightly clutching her purse.

Her eyes began to water, tears threatening to fall. She was deeply upset. "Oh, Jessie!"

"You must be Jessie's Mom. I'm Dr. Bartlett," he said calmly. "I'm just finishing up here. This is the last one."

He tied off the stitch and snipped the thread. "If the pain gets to be too much, she can have Ibuprofen which should help. If there are any problems, please don't hesitate to contact us. Are there any questions?"

"Yes," Mom said, her voice shaking. "Will be there any long term damage or scarring?"

"It's a simple cut. It will heal nicely. There may be a faint scar once the redness goes away. Other than that, she'll be fine."

"Oh!" she said, immensely relieved. "Thank you so much!"

"Not a problem. Have a good night." He nodded at me and then walked over to the next patient, picking up the chart, reading it as he approached the bed.

"Jessie, Ethan's father has kindly offered to pay for the hearing aid." Mom reached out and touched his shoulder, a silent gesture of thanks.

"Really?" I was stunned by his generous offer. "Thank You." It was all I could say.

"Ethan, we should go. It's getting late." He gripped Ethan's shoulder, encouraging him to get up.

Reluctantly, Ethan released my hand. "Bye Jess. I'll see you later, okay?" He nodded solemnly before turning away from me.

"Bye." I stared at him as he walked out the door.

"Are you ready to go? Is there anything you need?"

"I'm fine Mom." I got up, the sheets crinkling loudly, and pulled on my jacket. As we strode out into the lobby, she looked at my ear and bloody clothes, fussing with my shirt.

We drove home in silence. I looked out the window, my mind far away and numb.

CHAPTER 10

Leap of Faith

I was grateful I'd had the stitches taken out last week. They were itchy and drawing a lot of attention from everyone in the hallways. My classmates and teachers would stare openly at my bruised ear, apparently in shock, wondering what kind of monster would attack me so brutally. It was on days like that I was glad I couldn't hear the wild rumors going around. And just in time, too. The auditions were taking place at noon today as Amanda and Erica had so eagerly reminded me this morning.

While I walked down the noisy corridor, past the throngs of students as they slammed their lockers, chatter rising in a crescendo, I scanned for the familiar face of Dean, hoping to catch him and pass on the news.

I spotted him, glumly leaning against a locker, chewing on his pen as he listened to his pals banter back and forth.

"Dean!" I waved at him, trying to get his attention. "Dean!" I yelled a little louder, waving frantically. Finally noticing me, he pushed himself off the wall and took a step forward.

"Hi, Dean. Did you hear that the auditions are today at noon?"

He looked at me blankly, his response devoid of his usual pep.

"No. Why?" he said still munching on the cap of his pen.

"Seriously. I think it would do you a world of good if you came." I tried to be cheerful for him, but it was like talking to a sucking black hole of nothingness, pulling you into a swirling mass of negativity. "Please? For me? You have a better chance than I do at making this play," I pleaded. "This is my first time trying out for something like this."

He looked at me, not smiling much. "Okay. Where are we supposed to meet?"

Relieved I said, "Mr. Pringle's room just before noon."

We parted ways and went to our morning classes. My nervousness grew as the hour hand on the clock approached noon. I knew that I wanted to try something like this at least once in my life. I didn't want to regret not doing it for the rest of my life, filled with "what if's" or "why didn't I go for it?" This was an opportunity that I didn't want to pass up. I wanted to see how far I could go with it.

The bell rang at eleven forty-five. I grabbed my lunch bag from my locker and headed straight to Mr. Pringle's room upstairs. Mr. Pringle and I had never seen eye to eye since the day he told me that I couldn't take his music class because of my "disability."

I told him that I wanted to participate in his class like everyone else. Not once had he wavered in his decision, prompting me to wonder if he was the one who couldn't handle it.

I took a deep breath before stepping into his classroom, determined to prove to him that I could do it. As I crossed the doorway, I saw him sitting at his desk holding a chart in his hand. With his pinched features and puckered lips, he looked as if he had just sucked a lemon.

As he spotted me moving across the floor, his eyebrows arched near his receding hairline. He adjusted his glasses and sighed audibly as I approached him.

"I presume you are here for the audition?" he asked impatiently.

"Yes," I replied curtly, standing strong.

His jaw clenched tighter and I could see a vein throbbing on the side of his forehead.

"Please have a seat." He gestured toward the other students waiting near the back wall. My eyes roamed around the room at the sea of faces until I spotted Amanda and Erica chatting quietly, their heads close together. I strode over to them, and they squealed with delight once they saw me.

"Oh! Jessie! I'm so glad you made it!"

I muttered, "Thanks," feeling the butterflies in my stomach flutter out of control, threatening to escape.

My brows furrowed in concern as I looked around the room. "Have you seen Dean yet?"

They both shook their heads and went back to discussing choices of songs. I suddenly went rigid as I listened into their conversation. "Wait, wait—did you just say songs?"

Erica spoke first. "We are supposed to sing something for this audition."

My face paled and I put my hand on a nearby chair, feeling the room spin.

Amanda looked at me in alarm. "Jess? You okay?"

I stammered, still in shock, not really knowing what to say. "Sing? I can't sing! I don't know any songs! And you chose to wait until now to tell me this?!" My voice raised in pitch as I panicked.

"Seriously?" said Amanda, still concerned.

I threw a stony glare in her direction, not exactly liking her at this very moment, fuming, with my hand on my mouth in disbelief.

And that's when I saw Dean grace the doorway, walking slowly into the room. My heart rose in hope and I felt lighter, relieved that he had shown up. "Look! Dean's here! He made it!" I said to Amanda and Erica, momentarily forgetting my own dilemma.

It was just a few minutes later that Mr. Pringle began the auditions with some quick words and handed out a script to everyone, stopping to stare at me with a resigned sigh. His body language clearly conveyed irritation as he handed the sheet to me with a sharp flip of annoyance.

"Okay group. Here is what we are going to do now. I'm going to have six of you come up to the front of the class and run through this script." He looked at his chart. "The first group is Amanda, Brooklyn, Tiffany, Dean, Logan and Jessie."

My heart thudded in fear as we scampered to the front of the class, scripts in hand. I looked at my lines. They had a star beside them, indicating they were for my character.

Standing beside me was Tiffany, who was smiling like a blank Barbie doll, showing no fear whatsoever and actually enjoying this. I desperately wanted to smack that smile off her face.

Mr. Pringle spoke up. "Dean, go ahead and start with your character, Danny Zuko."

Dean started shyly at first but warmed up quickly, diving into the role. I stared at him in awe, thinking that he was a natural.

I tried to keep track of everyone speaking but couldn't lip read them and follow the script at the same time, thereby missing my cue. "Jessie?" Mr. Pringle was prompting me with his hand to hurry up and say my line.

"Sorry." I said my line quickly and did my best to keep up with the rest of the dialogue, missing my cue several times.

I could feel the tears brimming in my eyes as I realized how much of a failure I was at this.

"That's great. Now I want each of you to sing a few lines of a song in turn. Keep it short please." I clenched my hands feeling them sweat nervously.

I watched everyone sing confidently, feeling more nervous by the minute. Then it was my turn. I froze, my mind a complete blank.

"Jessie? It's your turn," said Mr. Pringle, arching his eyebrows at me, his pen poised above the clipboard.

"Um. I don't know any songs..." I fiddled with the script as I spoke, rolling and unrolling it in my hands.

"Fine. How about something simple like...'Twinkle, Twinkle Little Star'?" he suggested tersely.

I was terrified. My voice cracked at first, but I cleared my throat and sang the lullaby, feeling incredibly small. I could hear several people in the back snicker and saw some of them laughing behind their hands, their bodies shaking. My eyes started to burn again, tears threatening.

"And thank you. Have a seat."

I could feel the tears starting to fall. I strode out of the room, head hung low in shame, wiping them away with the sleeve of my shirt.

I walked around the hallways, gasping with shuddering breaths, as the scenario played in my mind over and over. I had no idea how long I walked around the school. I passed each room without comprehending where I was, staring blankly ahead of me.

I ended up in the cafeteria and realized that I didn't have my lunch bag with me. I dug through my pockets for some change and found that I had enough to get a drink and chocolate bar. I was starving and not thinking straight. I felt so numb at this point, I was glad to be doing something with my hands as I dropped the coins in the slot.

I yanked out the items from the bottom tray and strode to an empty table at the far end. I sat down, staring aimlessly at the people in the room. It was loud and incoherent with layers of conversations overlapping each other, making it impossible for me to hear anything.

I simply sat there, wondering what to do next when Amanda and Erica sat down beside me. "Hey, there you are, we looked all over the place for you."

They snapped me out of my reverie with their sudden announcement. "Huh? Oh, I was just walking around, getting a snack, you know."

"I'm sorry about Mr. Pringle He can be a bit of a prick at times," Erica said consolingly.

"Huh. No big surprise there. Guess he was right about me not being suitable for this type of stuff." I looked down at the table as I spun the empty juice bottle around in my fingers.

"That's not true. I thought you did fine. I fumbled my lines a couple of times," Amanda said, apparently trying to be helpful.

Erica smiled. "Hey, guess what? It looks like Dean got the part for Danny Zuko!" She seemed thrilled at the news.

I stared at her in surprise. "Seriously?"

"Yeah, no one else even came close to performing the role the way he did. He did a great job."

I nodded my head in agreement. "He did, didn't he? Well, I'm glad for him He needed this. How about you guys, any luck?"

They both shook their heads.

"I doubt it. Mr. Pringle hinted that it would likely be Tiffany or Brooklyn." Erica looked at her watch and announced that we should be getting back to our lockers.

We got up, and strode out of the cafeteria like the Three Musketeers, ready to forge ahead.

CHAPTER 11

Sway With Me

I held on to the kicking shield, keeping it firmly against my hip, as the younger kids kicked at it. They weren't any older than nine or ten and most of them wore white and yellow belts. They eagerly stood in line, thrilled at the opportunity to kick the crap out of me, and I blithely obliged, happy to help.

They were practicing their side kicks, staggering slightly as they raised their legs to deliver a blow, smiles as wide as their faces. Some of the girl's ponytails bounced up and down in time with their excited jiggling.

One of them lunged at me with a loud "Kiai," kicking the shield with a satisfying thud.

"Good job!" I said as he ran to the back of the line, giving high fives to his classmates.

Another one took his place, a slightly chubby young girl with freckles across her nose, and colorful braces like train tracks across her teeth. She leaned into the kick and her back leg gave out. She landed on the floor with a surprised thunk. She wasn't hurt, merely stunned.

"Wait! You can still kick at me from the ground. Go ahead and give it a try."

She looked up at me with a sly grin and struck the pad as hard as she could, happy to finish the kick.

Then all the other kids decided they wanted to do it from the ground, too. They cajoled me, with their pleas.

"Please? I wanna do it, too."

I looked at them, their eyes wide, as they bounced up and down and begged me.

I looked over my shoulder at Sensei Ethan and saw him watching me with an amused grin. I jerked my head at him, motioning him to come over and help. He put his hands to chest, saying silently, "Who, me?"

Then he strode casually over to me, glancing at the kids who switched to begging him. "Can we kick from the floor? Please Sensei Ethan?"

His smile grew into a broad grin, revealing perfectly white teeth, eyes crinkling at the corners with delight. "Sure, why not?"

"Should we use the gym mats so that they can all lie in a circle and I'll come at them with the shield? At least that way, it will be more unpredictable," I offered.

"Yep, great idea. Go for it," he replied. Then he turned to the students. "Okay guys, I want all of you to go grab a mat and place it on the floor."

They ran toward the wall where the blue gym mats were stacked and pulled them out, dragging them on the floor and laying them down flat.

Sensei Ethan gave me a slight punch in the arm. "That was awesome, thinking on your feet like that."

"Thanks," I said shyly.

I joined the kids as they pulled the last mat on to the floor and helped lock each strip, feeling the Velcro snap in place.

"All righty, everyone, lie on your left side in a big circle around me."

They sat down and rolled over onto their sides.

"This time, what I'll do is lunge at one of you. As soon as I come at you, I want you to do a side kick, as hard as you can into this shield. Are you ready?"

They bobbed their heads up and down, totally ready.

"Here I go!" I moved toward one of the girls, and she reacted quickly. I dashed toward one of the boys, but it took him a second to deliver a kick, surprised that I approached him so swiftly.

I continued going around the circle, back and forth, coming at them from different directions. Then I had them switch sides so that they could practice kicking with the other leg.

It was a great drill and they loved every minute of it.

After Sensei Ethan bowed them out and dismissed the class, I went to work cleaning up the dojo, putting the mats back against the wall, while he talked to some of the parents about areas that their kids could improve on or complimenting them on their progress.

We had come to an agreement that I would pay the portion of the monthly fee I could afford and cover the rest by assisting him or cleaning up the dojo, both of which I was happy to do.

He had told me that he knew I would become an instructor one day. Puzzled, I asked him how he knew. "It's hard to explain, you have leadership qualities, and you are great with the kids. That ability is there. I just see it. You pick up the techniques quickly and accurately. You work hard at it and excel at it. At this rate, I wouldn't be surprised if you became a black belt within the next couple of years.

"Plus I can feel it in my heart," he added injecting a very personal response.

"It's a long road but if we can get you started on learning how we run the classes, it will offer you more insight into what it is like to teach. Dad says you have amazing potential, and I agree."

He blew me away with his explanation. I was eager to be a part of this dojo and offered my assistance in any way I could.

I had a feeling that teaching ran in the family. My father was a professor and my older brother was a teaching assistant at his university.

After I put the mats away, I grabbed a broom and swept the floor, gathering up the bits of dust that floated into the corners. Then I picked up the rags and spray bottle, squirted the mirrors and began wiping them clean, occasionally checking for streaks. The mirrors stretched all the way across the wall, from the floor to the ceiling and I had stretch to reach the higher portions. It took a while for me to make my way across them all. By the time Ethan strolled back in, the parents and kids were gone.

He walked over to the radio, put a CD in its tray, and turned up the volume. Michael Buble's husky voice floated across the room and brought a smile to my face.

Ethan walked up to me, laid his hand on top of mine, and proceeded to move the rag in circular motions. I was surprised at his touch and I blushed.

We both looked past the rag, into the mirror, gazing at each other for a moment. I looked away, unsure of what to say or do. So I simply concentrated on cleaning the mirror with him, enjoying his other hand on my shoulder.

Sensing my shyness, he stepped away and started singing along with the song, "Kissing a Fool," lip syncing wildly, greatly exaggerating the emotions.

I burst out laughing, and tears formed in the corners of my eyes.

He continued to sing, using a large foam blocker, as long as my arm and twice as big around, as a giant microphone. With his hand on his heart, he sang, "I will wait for you...like I always have..."

It was hilarious. I slid down to the floor laughing.

The song faded away into a more upbeat rhythm. I stood up, euphoric from laughing so hard, and started to swirl around the room as the song, "Sway," played.

I danced across the floor, swaying back and forth, holding out the palm of my left hand with my right hand on top, using the sign language for "dance" and merging it into "with me."

I closed my eyes, feeling the beat and enjoying the song. Ethan embraced me from behind, placed his hands over the top of mine, signing along with me.

He sang along with the song, "Stay with me, sway with me," softly into my ear, his chin resting on my shoulder. Tenderly, we swayed to the music together, loving the moment.

He held me in a hug and I could feel his warmth around me like a cozy blanket, our connection to each other becoming stronger.

We stayed together like that for a few minutes, long after the song was over.

He grabbed one of my hands and spun me around, twirling me.

"So, are you ready for tomorrow?" I asked as I faced him.

"Tomorrow?" His brows creased then shot up as he remembered. "Oh, sure, the hockey thing. Yeah, I have my skates sharpened, ready to go."

"Cool. It will be mostly my cousins that will play with us. It's a great place. I used to spend all my afternoons during March Break out there. Just skating nonstop."

"Where exactly is it?" he asked curiously.

"It's not too far from where I live, just down the road. My mom will take us there so we won't have to walk all the way down there or back."

"What time did you want me to meet you?"

"My cousins will be there around one in the afternoon. Any time after that," I replied, looking forward to tomorrow.

"Great, I'll see you then," he said with a wink.

He turned around and looked at the clock on the wall. "Oops, it looks like your mom will be here any minute. You better get changed."

He was right. I dashed off to the changing room, stripped off my uniform and put on my clothes. I pulled on my socks and jacket, went by the door, and picked up my boots, yanking them on, pulling the laces snugly. Ethan leaned against the office desk, watching me, already changed.

The headlights of Mom's car came into view as she drove into parking lot. I waved goodbye to Ethan and went out the door as she came to a gentle stop in front of me.

The windshield wipers swished back and forth, batting away the slushy snow as we drove home in the darkness. Mom had the radio tuned into the weather station, listening for tomorrow's forecast. As she listened to the news, I stared out the window, remembering the tender moment when Ethan and I had swayed to the music.

It was late by the time we got home. I quickly ate supper and went upstairs to do some homework, hoping to get most of it out of the way before the weekend. I didn't relish the thought of working on it when I could be spending time outside with Ethan.

After a few hours hunched over my laptop, my eyes watering from staring at the screen for so long, I got up and stretched. Yawning, I made my to the bathroom, took a hot shower, put on my warm PJs, and snuggled into bed, thinking about tomorrow.

When I woke up, the sun was blazing its way through my bedroom window causing me to squint. I looked outside. The sky was a clear blue with the occasional fluffy cloud. A fresh layer of snow was everywhere. It appeared to be a gorgeous day so far.

I dressed quickly, grabbed my hockey bag and stick, thumped down the stairs, and dropped them by the door. I sat at the table with Mom as she passed the plate of pancakes and sausages over to me. Pouring maple syrup over everything, I dug in, savoring the sweetness of it.

In between bites, I asked Mom where Dad went today. "Oh, he went to visit his sister for the day." My aunt was also a professor and the two of them relished the opportunity to get together and exchange ideas about their research.

We flipped through the weekend newspaper as we sat beside the fireplace, enjoying the heat and crackling wood. She chose the business and local news, while I perused through the sports and entertainment sections, including the comics.

After a relaxing morning, I was glad when I spotted Ethan's father's car driving down the lane. I greeted them outside as Ethan stepped out of the car, wearing a heavy black jacket, thick fleecy pants and a toque.

"Hi, Ethan!" I called out as I picked up his bag and carried it over to Mom's car.

"Hey, Jessie! Great day, eh?" he replied.

Mom was standing beside his car, talking to his Dad for a few moments before walking back toward us.

We all piled into the car and went down the road toward a small lane, barely visible in the snow, with only a single set of tire tracks to follow. As we emerged through the thick woods, the trail opened up to reveal a valley with majestic hills in the background. If you squinted your eyes, you could almost imagine that they were snow-capped mountains instead.

In front of us was a large pond, a good portion of it cleaned off, the snow piled high on either side, creating natural walls that were reminiscent of a hockey rink. Two nets stood at either end of the pond, waiting patiently for the games to begin.

The scenery was stunning. It was practically an image right out of a Hallmark Christmas Card. There were already several people, armed with hockey sticks, skating on the ice, smacking the frozen puck around with glee.

As we got out of the car, I hauled my bag out of the truck, gave Ethan his bag, and pulled out our sticks at an awkward angle since it was a bit of a tight fit.

We marched down the pathway toward the base of a large tree where someone had the foresight to place a picnic table. We waved at Mom as she drove back through the lane, the tires crunching on the snow.

I threw my bag into the snow and started tugging off my boots. Ethan's eyes grew wide at the sight of my skates when I drew them out of the bag.

"Um, hang on. Aren't your skates supposed to be white?" he asked.

I looked up at him over my shoulder as I tugged on my laces. "Heh. Nope." I put on my helmet, snapping the chinstrap in place. Smirking, I pulled out my hockey gloves, tugging them on my hands. "You'll see why in a few minutes."

Once Ethan was finished doing up his laces, he pulled on his gloves, grabbed his stick, and marched toward the pond.

I jumped onto the ice with ease, enjoying the slick surface. I whizzed around Ethan, laughing with pure delight. "Come on!"

We met up with my cousins and I introduced them to him. "Hey guys! This is Ethan. Be nice to him."

"Ethan, this is Carter, Daniel, Jenny, and Cooper." I pointed at each of them as I said their names.

Their hands sat casually on top of their sticks, their cheeks were already rosy from being outside, and their breaths came out in puffs of air.

Carter spoke up. "Okay, Ethan you're with us, Jessie you're with Jenny and Daniel." I nodded and skated to the center of the ice.

Cooper and I stood at the face-off and battled over the puck. I managed to snag it from him and pass it back to Jenny. She glided around Ethan, deftly avoiding Carter, and passed it back to me. The two of us slid it back and forth and I shot the puck into the upper corner of the net.

"She scores!" yelled Jenny, giving me a high five.

"Great pass, Jenny!" I replied.

We went back to the face-off. I looked up at Ethan to see him staring at me in stunned disbelief. This time, Cooper got control of the puck, pulling it away from me, making a beeline to the net.

I skated toward him with the wind on my face, and an incredible sense of freedom.

I pushed my stick at Cooper's, trying to force it off. Turning around to face him, I skated backward in defensive mode.

I placed my body in front of his, deftly knocking the puck off his stick, swooped in, and picked it up, skating down the ice toward Ethan. Cooper was behind me, trying to catch up. Jenny raced alongside with me.

Ethan loomed in front of me. I quickly passed the puck to Jenny, did a deke to Ethan's side, and picked up the puck as she passed it back to me. We scored another goal, goading the guys. "Aw, what's the matter Coop? Can't keep up with us?"

We continued playing for another hour, soaking up the sun and crisp air. We yelled at each other in jest, enjoying the spirit of the game.

Ethan and I took a break and stood at the side of rink, panting from the exertion, steam visible with every breath we took. He skated up to me, threw his arm around my shoulders, pulling me close. "Sooo, when were you planning on telling that you played hockey?"

"What? You don't like the way I play?" I said, nudging him with my elbow, my hands sitting on top of my stick.

"Wow. And I mean, wow. You are good. I had no idea." He spoke earnestly, and seemed genuinely surprised.

I looked at my cousins who were dashing around one of the nets, trying to sneak a shot around Daniel.

"I used to play a couple of years ago but quit."

He sputtered. "W—why? You're so talented."

My throat constricted painfully. "I couldn't stand the way I was being treated. Even right from the beginning, it was pretty bad." I played with my stick, scooping up the snow with the curved blade.

"At one point, the coach didn't believe that I couldn't hear him. He thought that I was ignoring him on purpose. When I confronted him about it and showed him my hearing aids, he turned around and walked away. He never came back.

"The other coach was just as bad. He kept benching me even after I would ask him why he did it. He would do it every time I went offside. He would scream at me even though I couldn't understand a word he said on the ice, he was simply incoherent.

"Then as the year progressed, his attitude rubbed off onto the players. They started to treat me differently. One by one, they would stop passing the puck to me and wouldn't talk to me in the changing room."

Ethan watched me intently as I spoke. "By the end of the year, I couldn't take it anymore." I looked up into his eyes. "Remember those guys that went after me near the dojo a few months ago?"

He nodded, his brows furrowing.

"I played with their sisters. They were on my team..." I waited for him to figure it out.

He sucked in his breath as he made the connection. "Son of a—" His eyes grew wide. "Now it all makes sense." He gripped his stick tightly as he spoke, barely controlling his temper and leaned his forehead on his gloves in anger.

He shook off his gloves, hands shaking, and raked them through his hair. "Aw, Jess. They had no right to do that to you." He took a deep breath through his nose to calm down.

"Come here," he said, reaching out to pull me snugly to his chest, helmet and all.

CHAPTER 12

Whirlwind

S pring came swiftly, the snow melting as soon as the sun peeked out from behind the clouds. It was a gorgeous day, the lush grass practically glowing a deep green. The birds chirped nonstop, reaching a crescendo as it got warmer throughout the afternoon.

Classes went by like a blur, and I found them boring. Nothing seemed to grab my attention except the beautiful landscape outside the window. I kept glancing outwards, watching the birds flutter around the trees, wishing that I was out there with them.

I rifled through my locker, putting some books on the top shelf, others into my backpack, feeling the strap sink into my hand as it got heavier. I sniffed at my gym clothes, cringed and threw them in, too.

Satisfied I had everything I needed, I slammed the door shut and fastened the lock in place. I strolled down the hallway, pushing past the crowds as they too scrambled to catch the bus. I heard the PA system click on and a burst of unintelligible dialogue broke through the slamming of lockers and din of their voices. I had no clue what was said, but several of the students froze in alarm, fear etched on their faces.

Weird, I thought and continued down the corridor toward my bus, which was sitting on the roadway. They were all in a line like bright yellow beetles at a buffet. I could see them through the windows as I walked down the hallway.

I'd turned the corner and had my hand on the handle of the door when several of the teachers rushed past me. *What the—What is going on?* I wondered as I stepped outside. My bus was the first one in line, and I bounded up the stairs, spun around the metal pole, and sat down with a huff. The driver didn't even notice my entrance. He was so deeply occupied with the radio and glancing out the windows.

Several of the kids on the bus were chattering animatedly, abuzz with energy. Not all of them were excited though. Glenda looked visibly pale.

I shook my head thinking that all of this was rather odd. As I waited for the rest of the group to board the bus, I looked out the window on my right side and noticed that the sun was quickly being swallowed up dark clouds. Looks like it will rain soon, I thought.

I sat there wondering what was taking everyone so long. This bus was usually full by now.

Again the PA crackled to life, and once more I had no clue what was being said. The driver was talking rapidly to someone on the radio. I looked back at Glenda and I swore her face went another shade paler.

Okay, I'd had enough of being clueless. "Glenda, what did the PA say?"

She turned and pointed a shaking finger toward the windows on the left side of the bus where the sky was almost black, filled with swirling ominous clouds. Streaks of violent lightning shot downwards. I had never seen a storm look like that before.

And it was rapidly coming this way.

All Glenda could utter was, "Tornado."

Incredulous, I scoffed at her. "Yeah, right. Like you expect me to believe that." After being ridiculed all year long by my classmates pulling pranks on me relentlessly, I had reached the point of not being able to trust anyone.

Just as I spoke those words, Mr. Wilson stomped up the stairs and onto the bus with a frantic look on his face, watching the stormy sky over the driver's shoulder. He turned toward us and urged us to get off right away and go back into the school.

"Oh come on! I just got on!" I exclaimed.

He threw a stern look my way, sharply pointed his finger out the door and said, "Now."

As he ushered us back into school, I was stunned to find that everyone was being forced back into school.

As he guided all of us back through the doors into the hallway, Mr. Wilson yelled at my group, "Get back to your homeroom class now!"

The lights flickered, bringing a chorus of gasps within the hallway. Several of us walked into the classroom, looking confused. Suddenly a door slammed shut, making us all jump. Our nerves were raw by now. Most of us sat down in the chairs and watched the squall through the large wall of windows. It provided us with a frightening view of the intense power of the storm. The leaves shook violently. The trees bent so far over that the branches were nearly touching the ground. Hail pounded against the glass, making a loud and relentless clattering noise. Flashes of lightning streaked into the classroom with massive claps of thunder, shaking the tables. The deep rumbles vibrated through the floor.

The sky turned a shocking emerald green and the windows started to rattle. "What the hell?" I got up to look out the window when Mr. Wilson burst into the room and yanked on my arm, ripping the fabric of my shirt sleeve, pulling me away from windows.

"Everyone get away from the windows!" His face was etched with fear. I had never seen him scared before and chills suddenly ran down my spine.

All of us jumped out of our seats and scrambled toward the walls, not feeling much safer. The lights blinked out, plunging us into darkness. Thereby also sending my heart into deep shock. I was scared out of my mind. My heart thumped wildly. It took a minute before the emergency lights kicked in, but they were only able to cast a feeble glow within the room.

The lightning flashed through the window with fierce intensity, nearly blinding us as the hail continued to pound against the glass.

"Okay! Everyone go out into the hallway, turn left and then right, down the stairs to the basement." He gestured at us frantically to leave the room. We scampered out as fast as we could and all I could do was follow the wave of students being channeled down the stairs.

It was utterly confusing as I could barely hear the teacher's directions over the cacophony of the thunder, hail, and the noisy chatter of the students.

There was another loud bang as a door slammed shut. We all froze, shocked into silence. When we finally reached the bottom of the stairs, it was darker and smelled dank and musty. In the dim light, I could see rows of pipes running along the ceiling.

There were several more bangs, everyone flinched. We were packed into the long hallway like sardines, terribly cramped.

Suddenly the roar intensified. I could feel deep vibrations through my chest. The hair on the back of my neck reared up. In the faint glow from the exit sign, I could see how frightened everyone looked, as they cast glances upward at the ceiling. I put my hand on the wall to steady myself and immediately felt the effects of the rumbling. I gasped in horror as I realized that the walls were shaking. The wind howled upstairs.

I could hear the teachers talking to us but I had no idea what they were actually saying since I couldn't see their faces, which scared me. Despite being surrounded by my classmates and teachers, I felt utterly alone.

The rumbling grew substantially louder and I now could feel the vibrations beneath my feet. Suddenly there was a huge explosion of noise and the crowd ducked down in reflex, some pushing in my direction, as plumes of dust and debris tumbled down the stairs.

Screams pierced the air. We all immediately covered our heads as we knelt on the floor. I was shaking so hard I couldn't stop my teeth from clattering.

We stayed down, crouched in fear, for what seemed like an eternity, waiting for the rumbling to subside.

Gradually, we stood up, confident it was almost over. I could see a couple of the teachers talking on their cell phones, others peering up the stairs and tentatively stepping around the debris.

The quiet murmurs grew to a chatter as we waited for the all-clear from our teachers. A figure came pounding down the stairs, looking pale, talking on the phone, beckoning the other teachers to gather around.

Finally they broke apart from their group and faced us. "Okay folks, it's safe to go back upstairs. Please watch where you walk and go directly to your homeroom."

The crowd began to inch forward up the stairs, past shattered bricks and debris sprinkled liberally on the floor. The closer we got to the top, the thicker the debris became, strewn with pieces of wood, torn posters, ripped books, wet leaves and branches, all crunching beneath our feet as we walked. Glass glittered on the floor. Rivulets of water flowed down the wall, trickling onto the floor.

It was a shocking sight as we emerged from the stairwell. The sky was no longer dark. As a matter of fact, brilliant sunshine lit up the rooms, revealing the destruction all around us. Windows were shattered. Their panes hung limp and broken Water continuously dripped down the wall. Doors were nearly ripped off their hinges, hanging askew, barely holding on.

Most shocking of all, the section of the wall, where we had come through from the buses, was gone. The front doors didn't exist anymore. In their place was one of the buses, rudely slammed sideways into the bricks. Pieces of the wall crumbled and clattered to the floor.

We stood in awe at the extensive damage. We had been on those buses not too long ago.

Mr. Wilson rushed into the classroom. He surveyed the damage and told us to pick up our backpacks. He cautioned us not to sit on anything due to the glass that littered every surface and crunched beneath our feet.

"You are to wait here until we can get the buses organized and get you all home," he said as we stared out the broken windows, stunned speechless.

CHAPTER 13

Appleby Estate

I t took me a while to get used to the rain again. My fear of storms was deeply rooted after the tornado we had last month. I twitched at the sight of dark clouds, waiting for them to turn green at any moment. It was ridiculous to feel so insecure. Although the weather has been amazingly cooperative lately, gracing us with dazzling sunshine and warm temperatures for the weekend, I was still uneasy.

I spent a long morning in the dojo, helping Ethan with the young children. The first two hours were divided into two groups, the beginners and the advanced. I held onto the kicking shields, stood by their side as they walked on the low balance beam, practicing their kicks, and obtained various pieces of equipment for the instructors upon their request.

The last class was for the instructors to work on their own requirements and refine their skills. Since I was not officially part of the teaching program, I could not participate in this class along with them.

While they focused on their katas and fancy footwork, it gave me the opportunity to practice my form in the spacious lobby. I concentrated on my blocks and strikes, moving swiftly. I wanted to do a good job for my next grading, which was coming up soon. I had found that practicing my katas repeatedly helped me feel comfortable with it. Occasionally I stopped to take a short break and watch the instructors deliver stunning flying kicks that left me breathless and impressed with their desire to learn even more advanced moves.

It took a lot of effort to pull my eyes away from their mesmerizing style and speed, but I went back to working on my kata, feeling a bit clumsy compared to them. After they were finished and bowed out, everyone proceeded to their respective locker rooms. Before I reached the door, Ethan called out my name, reaching for me. "Wait a sec, Jessie." His hazel eyes shone brightly, nearly green in this light which gave him a dreamy look.

"Sure. What's on your mind?" I looked up at him, waiting for his response.

His forehead creased in concentration. "I really don't know how to say this..."

Suddenly I was infused with a shock of cold fear. "Did I do something wrong in class?"

His eyes grew wide then he relaxed as he realized how I came to that conclusion.

"Oh, no! You didn't do anything wrong. I just wanted to ask you a question." He appeared suddenly shy, looking down at his belt, fiddling with the ends.

"I was wondering if you would like to come back to my place for the afternoon. It's such a great day and it would be a shame to spend it indoors." He gestured toward the large windows, the bright sun gleaming off the mirrors and floor.

I thought about it. He was right. It would be awesome to spend some time outside. My eyes lit up, thrilled to be asked to visit his home. "Yeah. I would love to!"

Relief suffused his face and his shoulders visibly relaxed. "Cool. I'll see you in a few minutes." And he dashed off to the locker room.

I made my way to my own locker room and quickly took off my uniform. I pulled on my shamrock green hoodie and jeans, excited at the prospect of seeing his home for the first time. I threw everything in my sports bag and slung it over my shoulder.

He was already by the door, smiling sweetly. "I'll take that for you." He pulled my bag off my shoulder as I bent down and put my shoes on, tugging at the laces. As I stood up, he held out his arm like a perfect gentleman. I laughed, loving his old-fashioned manners.

His father drove up while Ethan locked the dojo. He opened the back door, ushered me in, and placed our bags in the trunk, slamming it shut, and slithered in on my left side. His eyes twinkled with delight, his face practically glowing in the sunlight.

The car itself was luxurious and remarkably clean, possibly the cleanest one I had ever seen. It screamed luxury and pure comfort. It reminded me of the cars I had seen on James Bond movies, like the fancy Aston Martins.

He turned to face me, straining against the seat belt, as if anxious to engage in a conversation. It was obvious he was trying to contain his enthusiasm. I could see Ethan's father peeking in the rear view mirror watching us, eyes crinkling as if he was amused.

Before Ethan could speak, I had a question I wanted to ask, "So, do you attend school around here? I haven't seen you at my school at all."

He titled his head to the side and paused, as if he had to think about it. "Ah...not really. You see, I go to a more exclusive school in a private location. It's a thirty minute drive from here."

Curious, I pressed further. "Wait, do you mean a private school?"

He nodded briefly, "Yeah, it's a beautiful place. Very old fashioned and stuffy at times, you know kinda like Hogwarts from Harry Potter."

Damn, I thought, that's totally cool. "Wow. Lucky you. My parents could never afford that. They really wanted to enroll me, but it just wasn't possible."

His father spoke up, looking at me in the mirror. "Go on Ethan, tell her what you do for fun," he said grinning mischievously.

"Dad!" he admonished and I could swear that he blushed slightly. He briefly looked out the window, collecting his thoughts, then looked back at me. "Heh. Um. I'm a fencer."

I blinked my eyes rapidly, caught off guard. I wasn't expecting that at all. "Seriously?" I was sure my face displayed shock. "That's incredible. I have never met anyone who did that. What's it like?"

"Well, it's challenging, not only physically but also mentally. It's not as easy as it looks. In a way, it's like a game of chess where you have to try to predict what your opponent will do."

I tried to imagine him wearing the outfit, holding the foil, and delivering the winning strike. It boggled my mind. It was like a different world to me.

I looked past his shoulders and could see that the landscape changed from the crowded cityscape to a lush countryside, trees lining the sides of the roads, blooming in bright fluffy sprouts. It seemed like the trees had exploded overnight, suddenly filled with leaves.

"Where are we?" I said as Ethan followed my line of sight.

"This is Maple Grove Valley."

"It's so lush. I've never been here before."

He exchanged a brief glance with his father who was listening in.

"It's quiet out here and immensely private. We don't have very many neighbors around us."

I looked over my shoulder, surprised that we'd passed a vineyard. I jerked my thumbed in that direction, "Was that a vineyard?"

"Yep. Dad is the owner of that vineyard. It was his idea to try it here. An old pal of his from Italy runs it for him."

My head started to spin, first the fancy car, private school, fencing, and now a vineyard? Who were these people? I was starting to get nervous, feeling a bit out of place.

Then the car slowed down and turned left into a secluded gravel driveway. We passed thick bushes, heavy woods on either side, and the occasional open field. It was nearly half a mile long. The tires crunched on the gravel.

In front of us appeared two tall stone columns embracing the driveway with an elaborate wrought iron gate decorated with the letter A. On the column was a sign with the words, "Appleby Estate." We drove onto a private estate surrounded by lush green lawns.

It was a circular path. We slowly went past a large pond complete with a spouting fountain in the center, surrounded by a canopy of willow trees. We came to a stop in front of a huge manor beautifully finished with gray stones and smooth marble columns.

In front was a graceful floral garden with a simple walkway that gently curved toward the entrance. I sucked in my breath, feeling as if I'd entered another world. It was the kind of scenery I had only seen in magazines.

Ethan had his hand on the door handle. "Come on, let's go for a walk. I'll give you a tour."

I stepped out of the car and Ethan beckoned me toward the pond. We walked side by side as I absorbed the dazzling surroundings. The willow trees formed an elegant circle around the pond, their long slender branches flowing downwards like fingers reaching out to touch the water. Their leaves, swayed gently in the breeze.

A frog leaped in the air in front of my foot, diving into the pond and sending ripples across the surface as the sun danced merrily on the rims.

Birds, lots of them, could be heard twittering all around me. Several butterflies were fluttering around the bushes resplendent with pink blossoms. It was simply jaw dropping and all I could think was, "pinch me."

We walked in silence for a few minutes. Ethan watched my reactions, smiling. He slid his hand down my arm, merging his fingers with mine.

I breathed in deeply, inhaling the scent of freshly cut grass and sweet spring air. Just around the bend of the pond, to my left was a simple wooden bench.

"This place is amazing. How long have you lived here?" I said as I sat down on the bench with Ethan. My eyes wandered everywhere, taking in the sights. All around the property were tall trees with large branches that swayed in the breeze. The dense trees looked ancient and strong creating a natural fence all around us. At the very top of one of the trees stood a rich black Raven, cawing out to its young who were hopping up the branches, one at a time toward the top.

"We've been here for most of my life," Ethan replied, watching the birds. "My parents moved here when I was still quite young, perhaps three or four."

"Wow. It feels so safe here, very peaceful."

"Yes, that's one of the reasons why they picked this spot." He nodded, his hair an even lighter shade in the sun. "Speaking of peaceful, there is a garden here that I should show you."

Suddenly a bright orange cat burst out from under a nearby bush, leaping just onto the edge of the pond.

"Oh! He's adorable!" I said, briefly startled. Then I relaxed as I gazed at the cat.

Laughing, Ethan said, "That's Saffron. She's quite the hunter and fiercely protective of me. She follows me whenever I'm outside."

We watched her pounce on a frog, giggling, as she followed the frog hopping across the lawn, leaping whenever it leaped. Her eyes were sparkling and her tail swished playfully, clearly absorbed in this game. When the frog wouldn't budge, she would softly touch it with her paw, encouraging it to leap so that she could continue to follow it.

"Come on, there is so much to see!" Ethan pulled on my hand gently, his fingers still intertwined with mine.

We strolled further toward the back of the extensive property where there was a large vegetable garden and archway beside it. The archway was covered with grapevines, weaving elaborately through the trellis.

The ground in the garden was freshly dug up with visible rows and tall blank markers that sat at the end of each row, waiting to be labeled. "This is my father's favorite spot. He enjoys gardening and is always trying out something new every year. Last year, he was able to grow baby watermelons and tiny white pumpkins."

Ethan pointed out the area as he spoke. "This year he is considering trying to grow Spaghetti Squash and Purple Royal Potatoes."

"Sounds like he enjoys the challenge, particularly since winter is so harsh around here."

Ethan nodded. "Yep, it really inspires him to do something new each time."

"Over here is one of my mother's favorite spots." He pointed toward a stone walkway that led toward the other side of the house. We walked in silence on the green grass as the sound of gurgling water became stronger. Within minutes I saw the source—a river that followed the length of the property. It was at least ten feet wide and went for miles in either direction. It bubbled and frothed along the edges, rolling over the stones as it flowed past me.

The section where we stood was busy, but I could see that it was calmer further down. Curious I asked, "Are there any fish in there?"

As soon as the words were out of my mouth, a large one leapt out of the water and landed with a splash, leaving a ring of ripples.

"Yep," Ethan responded in jest.

I rolled my eyes at his remark. "Never mind..."

We veered up toward the stairs, where dozens of ferns uncurled, fingers stretching out on either side. Another sweet fragrance floated nearby. I frowned not finding the source. "What's that lovely smell?"

Looking around, Ethan seemed puzzled for a moment then realized what I was interested in. "Ah. That would the Lilly of the Valley. They have tiny white flowers that look like bells. There are some up here." He pounced up several steps, bent down, and plucked a few from the base of the ferns.

"Here." He handed me the delicate strand covered with white little upside down cups with frilly edges. "Their smell is intoxicating."

I sniffed at them, loving their scent. "They are so cute!"

We neared the top of the stairs where the surface was covered in tiny smooth pebbles and every foot or so there was a large flat stone, creating a pathway. It was a very different type of garden from any I had ever seen. On my right, there were several small trees with tiny red leaves unfurling. It looked like a miniature maple tree.

Along the edge of the pathway were dozens of white roses covered in red streaks as if someone took a paintbrush and splattered them decoratively. To my left were tall bamboo stalks and ornamental grass with green and white stripes.

In the center of this unusual garden was a large Japanese stone lantern. Behind it were two curved stone benches along the pathway leading toward it.

"My mother loves to sit out here and listen to the river. She finds it to be a calming influence."

"It's a Japanese garden isn't it?" I said as I stepped on the large stones, following the path and reaching out to touch the leaves on the red maple tree.

He nodded in response.

We were now looking out over the river and I could see a bridge in the distance crossing over to a small island.

We took a few steps down into an elegant courtyard, complete with an outdoor fireplace, and several concrete benches jutting out from the wall. There was an entranceway to the house on my left side. It looked like it was an extension of the house, perhaps a sun room with large windows all around it.

It was beautiful to be up here like this, and I could easily imagine the family sitting out here in the summer, having lovely lunches or an afternoon tea.

"I'm speechless Ethan. This is amazing," I said as we stood by the stone wall watching the river trickle by.

He beamed and ruffled his hair with his hand. "Yeah. We often have cookouts here in the summer. It's perfect for roasting hot dogs and marshmallows.

"I should show you the front yard which is just up ahead and around the corner." He led me past the stone fireplace, complete with a tall chimney, toward a clearing of immense green lawn and several more flower beds. The ground slanted beneath my feet and I realized that we walking on a gentle slope back down to the level of the river.

As we strolled toward the front, there was an intriguing scent filling the air. We passed a small bushy tree adorned with bundles of tiny purple flowers. I leaned in to savor its delightful scent.

"This is a lilac tree. We also have a white one over here." He gestured behind the tree that was hidden from view.

"They're lovely. Their scent is quite strong!"

At that moment, Saffron came trotting over to see us, carrying a large feather in her mouth. She came to a stop at my feet and placed the feather on the grass. "Oh thank you Saffron. You're so sweet!"

I bent down and scratched her soft, furry forehead as she glanced up at me with her plump cheeks and proud smile.

Ethan grinned. His hands in his pockets, he rocked on his heels. "I think it's a gift for you. It's her way of saying hello."

"Aw. Can I pick her up?"

"Sure," he said, watching me scoop her up into my arms. She immediately started purring, rumbling loudly, leaning her head into my chin.

"Shall we go this way?" He gestured slightly to the left in front of the house. In the middle of the vast lawn was a large circular garden, filled with a variety of plants sprouting upward. Many of them were starting to open, displaying a multitude of colors. In the center was a simple birdbath on a tall column filled with water and a couple of small birds sitting on the edge.

We strolled casually onto the flat stone pathway that appeared in front of us as we approached the house. It wound in a gentle curve toward the front steps, the grass peeking through the gaps in the stones.

Ethan reached the steps first and stretched forward to pull the open the screen door. I could smell a tantalizing aroma that reminded me of Italian restaurants.

It smelled delicious and my mouth was already watering. Once I stepped into the kitchen, Saffron jumped down from my arms onto the soft beige ceramic floor.

To my right was a long wooden dining room table, surrounded by simple straight backed chairs. Behind the table was a freestanding countertop, with a couple of cutting boards on top, knives tucked to one side, filled with chopped tomatoes and herbs.

Beveled white cabinets ran around the wall overtop an L shaped counter with a sunken large double sink. An oven and refrigerator stood at the far end. There were several people in the kitchen area, moving briskly and in the middle of preparing a meal.

"Mmm. What smells so good in here? I'm practically drooling," I told Ethan.

He pointed to the various individuals by the counter. "Grandma Rose is making fresh Ravioli," he said, gesturing toward an energetic elderly lady, her white hair cut in a short bob. I could see that she wore hearing aids as well.

She glanced my way, smiling, as Ethan spoke. She wore a turquoise blue polo and crisp denim capris, it was a simple yet snappy outfit and it suited her well.

Ethan gestured toward the younger woman standing beside his father. "Standing beside Dad is Mum, her name is Katrina but everyone calls her Katie."

She glanced up from mixing the salad and wiggled her fingers in a little wave. She wore a creamy white polo and a black tennis skirt that showed off her fit legs.

Ethan's father was peeking in the oven behind her and based on the aroma that floated my way, he was checking the garlic bread.

His Mum spoke up. "Ethan, could you please set up the table for me? I think lunch is almost ready."

"Sure." Ethan grabbed a stack of plates sitting on the counter and carried them over to the table, placing them in front of each chair.

"Here, you can do the utensils and napkins." He handed them to me as he went around the table.

While I helped, I took the opportunity to admire the kitchen. It felt comfortable and lived in. It had an old world feel to it, with its honey colored walls and ceramic tiles along the counter. I could easily imagine Ethan doing his homework on this very table.

As I folded the napkins and tucked them beside the plates, Saffron surprised me by peeking out from beneath the table. Sitting on the chair watching me, she looked very regal and ready to eat lunch along with the rest of us. I laughed as I spotted her there. She looked right at home.

"You don't by any chance have a little plate for Saffron, do you?" I said pointing at the empty spot on the table in front of her.

"Ha! No. I suppose I should, eh?"

Just as Ethan and I finished setting the table, everyone came over carrying plentiful bowls and dishes of appetizing food. His father placed the large platter of garlic bread in the center of the table, beside the red bowl of steaming Ravioli. Katie put down a clear glass bowl of what looked like Caesar salad.

Ethan reached out for a chair on my right and gestured for me to sit in it. As I sat down, he took the chair beside me, smiling shyly. I suddenly felt very shy being in his house for the first time. Even though I knew his father, it felt strange to be with him outside of the dojo.

This was a different world for me, especially since I was seeing another side of Ethan and his father.

His father sat at the end of the table on my left side, his Mum and Grandma sat across from us. Saffron, of course, sat at the other end watching us from her spot, her whiskers practically on the table, her nose twitching as the scents floated around.

We each took turns dishing out the salad, and passing around the garlic bread then dug into our meal.

The Ravioli was scrumptious. I could taste the fresh Basil and cheese in it. "This is really good!" I gestured at the pasta, swallowing at the same time.

I could see a big grin form on Grandma Rose's face. She looked too young to be a Grandmother. I always thought a Grandma was supposed to wear an apron with their hair up in a bun.

"Grandma Rose made it from scratch. That's why it tastes so good." Ethan spoke in between mouthfuls of garlic bread.

"Seriously? How long does it take to make?" I said looking at Grandma Rose.

She smiled. "Not long dear, it's all second nature to me."

"My mom would love this! She's a caterer and she's always cooking up a storm." I could just see her trying out this recipe, tasting the sauce from the spoon.

"I would love to meet her sometime, perhaps we could swap recipes," she responded, scooping up the Ravioli.

I nodded. "I definitely could see the two of you together doing just that."

Grandma Rose seemed curious. "What type of catering does she do?"

"Oh...um. Small weddings, office parties, special events like grand openings." I thought about what she was really good at and decided it was desserts. "Her talent lies in desserts. She makes amazing cupcakes with cute little flowers on top. They're my favorite."

"She must be awfully busy doing all of those events," mused Grandma Rose, stabbing her fork into the salad.

"Yeah, she is actually. She tries to be at home more often but it's not easy and we need the money." I said. I looked down at my plate as I spoke the last few words, moving the food around my plate.

Sensing an awkward moment, Katie spoke up. "I love the color of your hearing aids!"

"Thanks. So do I. It wasn't easy picking the color. I really wanted pink but it wasn't available." I pouted recalling the disappointment that the one color I adored I couldn't have.

"But it's worth it to wear such bright colors. I learned the hard way that it turns it into a more positive experience, especially with people who don't know me. It's a great way to break the ice.

"Last month, I was shopping at the mall and had trouble hearing the salesclerk, it wasn't until she saw them that she realized I couldn't hear her. She apologized and slowed down, speaking clearly and was nicer to me. It really helped with the situation and I was grateful that she saw them."

I smiled as I recalled another incident. "Last year, at the beginning of the school year, one of my classmates noticed them and made the strangest remark." I paused for a second, gathering the words.

"He said to me 'Hey I didn't know you wore hearing aids—you're younger than my grandmother!'"

Everyone at the table chuckled. Ethan asked, "What did you say to him?"

"I was so surprised that all I could say was 'Gee thanks, I think.' At least he walked away with a more open mind."

Grandma Rose leaned on the table, delighted with the topic. "You know, now that you mention it, I have had people acting strangely sometimes when I don't hear them either. I think it's because they don't realize I can't really can't hear them, as opposed to being rude or ignoring them."

She leaned toward Katie. "Maybe I should consider getting fun colors like hers someday, eh?"

Katie nodded, apparently liking the idea, and then faced me as she asked, "What colors do they come in?"

"It's a virtual rainbow, although it really depends on the company that makes them. The manufacturer of my hearing aids tend to stick with primary colors as well as translucent purple, see through blue, or peek a boo green like mine. The newest addition to their line is the metallics—bronze, silver, black. And of course the usual icky assortment of plain beige, boring white, and dull brown."

I could see both of them considering their options, intrigued by the choices.

As we continued munching on our salad and crunchy garlic bread, I pondered what it must have been like for

Ethan growing up. This kitchen felt downright cozy, a perfect place for them to gather together at the end of the day and trade stories.

Jonas broke the silence. "So, what are your plans for the rest of the day?"

Ethan grinned. "That's easy—hang out, give Jessie the grand tour, show her the beach house." I perked up upon hearing the words beach house, thinking my hearing aid batteries were on the verge of dying and I heard wrong.

"Wait. Did you say beach house?" I asked, perplexed and curious.

Ethan shot me an impish smile. "Yep. I was going to show it to you later on today."

I began to wonder if he was up to something.

His father spoke again. "It's on the other side of the river, on the little island. It's hard to see from over here since there are so many trees. There is a bridge that will take you across the river."

Katie chimed in. "It's lovely dear. You'll like it. We use it as mini get away for those days when we want to just read a book or play games. It's also a guest house for our family and friends."

"It's cute. It's like a little B&B," added Grandma Rose.

I couldn't wait to see it. "Why do you have two houses? This one seems quite large."

"Ah! Actually, the previous owners were going to move to a retirement home out West to be closer to their family and offered us a chance to buy the property from them. We said yes and decided to change it into a beach house for our guests," Ethan's father pitched in.

Grandma Rose stood up and started gathering our plates. "I'll help," I said picking my plate as well as Ethan's.

As I started to walk toward the counter, I noticed Ethan and his father leaning toward each other, whispering, casting a glance my way.

"Why, thank you, dear," Grandma Rose said as I placed the plates by the sink.

"Say, would you like to help me bake some cookies? I could use a helping hand decorating them."

"Sure." I was looking forward to spending time with them. They embraced me like family. It was turning out to be a great day.

"While you ladies spend some quality time together, Ethan and I have some work to do outside. It shouldn't take too long." Jonas steered Ethan out the door, letting it close with a bang.

Ethan looked over his shoulder and said loudly, "Have fun!"

Those two are indeed up to something, I thought, it must be a guy thing.

As Grandma Rose quickly mixed the cookie dough, from scratch of course, Katie handed me the powdered sugar, sprinkles in neon pink and lime green, and several cookie cutters in the shape of heart and flowers. We spent the next hour gossiping and laughing while we baked the cookies.

I was spreading pink sprinkles over the iced cookies when Ethan came back in. He strode over to the racks of cookies, snatched one up and eagerly munched it, smiling.

He turned around, held out his arm, extending his open hand toward me. "Ready for the rest of the tour?" He quickly grabbed another cookie as I picked up one for myself and reached for his hand.

He led me through the house, going upstairs and down the hallway, walking on simple wooden floors, introducing me to various rooms, including his bedroom, which had its own balcony overlooking the sparkling pond.

We stood on the balcony, leaning against the railing, relaxing and enjoying the scenery.

"Your mom and grandma were really nice to me. I had a great time with them."

He nudged me with his elbow and winked at me. "I think they like you too. Who knows? Maybe they'll adopt you."

"Which reminds me...what were you and your dad up to earlier?"

"Huh? Oh, you mean the outdoorsy stuff? You'll see soon enough." Again he smiled impishly.

"What to continue the tour?" he asked facing me, his hand on the railing. His other hand reached out and twirled a strand of my curly hair around his fingers.

"That would be great. There is so much to see!"

We strode off the balcony, hand in hand, through the living room toward the sun room.

The sun room reminded me of a greenhouse. It was filled with pots of bushy plants and flowers. Some sat on small elegant tables. Others hung from hooks in front of the floor to ceiling windows.

"So I hear that you used to carry around a stuffed elephant when you were younger." I remarked. The conversation between his Mom and Grandma had been a treasure trove of delightful tidbits like his nickname. It was a very revealing bake-a-thon which satisfied my sweet tooth and curiosity about this side of him.

He rolled his eyes, sighing in disgust upon hearing about his childhood. "I see that they been forking over our family secrets."

"Oh yeah, some of it was very interesting and um, shall we say, revealing?"

He snorted in response, clearly more interested in moving on.

"Speaking of revelations, shall we continue on outside?" he said, opening the door for me and venturing back out to the stone patio.

We strolled alongside the river in the deep grass as we made our way toward the bridge.

CHAPTER 14

Memories

We sat side by side on the bridge, our legs swinging back and forth off the edge, watching the river churn beneath us. The scent of violets wafted through the air. There was a patch of tiny yellow and purple violets on the lawn not too far from us. It was a lazy afternoon, the sun high in the sun, warming our faces.

I sneaked a glance at Ethan, happy to be with him on such a beautiful day. He caught me looking at him and chuckled. "What? Is there something on my face?"

I laughed, surprised at his reaction. "No. It's just that it has been such a great day. It's perfect." I inhaled deeply, "I love the smell of those flowers. They are so sweet."

His eyes crinkled a little bit at the corners, sparkling in the sunlight. "Ah. Don't tell my mother that. Those flowers drive her crazy, they grow like weeds."

"Really? Wow, I never would've guessed."

He turned his head, resting it on his forearm. Reaching out with his other hand, he pulled a stray lock of hair out of my eyes and tucked it behind my ear. We stared at each other for a moment, our gazes locked.

He spoke up first. "Jessie?" Then he stopped. He seemed almost embarrassed.

"What?" I asked, wondering why he hesitated.

"This may seem awkward and I'll understand if you don't answer."

Even more curious, I replied, "Well go ahead, it's okay."

Appearing to gather his courage, he said, "I was wondering...how did you lose your hearing?"

Aha. I'd wondered when he would get around to asking that question. It was always in the back of my mind, lurking in the dark, waiting to rear its ugly head.

Suddenly uncomfortable, I briefly looked away, toward the frothy steam below.

He interrupted my thoughts. "You know what, don't worry about. Just ignore everything I said okay?"

"No, it's okay." I looked back at him, feeling both afraid and confident at the same time. I was five. I became quite ill with Meningitis. I don't remember much but I do recall spending a lot of time at home. I missed several months of school, which set me back a year." As I spoke, the memory became stronger, as if it was right in front of me.

"Mom acted strange, uncertain. She seemed nervous around me which frightened me. I couldn't figure out what was going on. There were days when she sat beside my bed reading books to me and I couldn't understand what she said."

I took a moment to take a breath and collect my thoughts. "She seemed terrified as if she lost something."

Ethan tilted his head, listening intently.

So I continued, remembering long forgotten details. "Apparently that's when I lost my hearing. The funny thing is, I don't remember anything before that. I have no idea what things are really supposed to sound like. I can't remember what my voice sounded like then."

As if reflecting my mood, a cloud drifted over the sun, casting a shadow on us. I shivered briefly at the sudden coolness.

"My parents, well, mostly my mother, took courses to learn sign language."

His brows drew together. "Wait. Why did they have to know sign language? You can obviously hear with the hearing aids."

"Not really. I can only hear an average of maybe half of any spoken conversation. Without my hearing aids, I hear absolutely nothing."

I could see that he was going to ask another question so I quickly finished my tale. "You see, I don't wear them all the time. I take them out at night and usually don't wear them in the morning or on the weekends."

He looked confused. "But why? Why would you leave them out?"

I smiled, amused by his question. "Well, it gets tiring. I work so hard at trying to follow conversations at school. Don't forget that I rely on a lot of lip reading and watching body language. There is always a lot going on at the same time so it's easy to miss something, especially if someone turns away from me or it's really noisy, like in the gym.

"I have to pay attention just to keep up with everyone else. By the end of the day, I'm worn out. By the weekend, I can't take it anymore. It's like an overload on my body.

"When I was much younger, I was often behind in social skills which made it seem like I was mentally slower than the rest of my classmates. It was ironic, since I was smarter than most of them. I just couldn't hear well enough to keep up."

He nodded. "I can see that, in some ways I know you're smart but also a little bit different. Don't take this the wrong way, but there are days when you seem to be a million miles away in deep thought." He paused for a moment. "I can't explain it. It's like you keep everything close to your chest for some reason."

I blinked rapidly, wondering what prompted this sudden change in our conversation. I narrowed my eyes at him. "Um...what just happened here? You just went way off topic all of a sudden."

A horrible thought dawned on me. "Did someone from school talk to you recently?"

He must have seen the stricken look on my face. "What? Oh, no, not at all. Oh, God, that's not I meant." He sighed. "I was afraid you would take this the wrong way. What I meant was that you are different than most girls I know." He reached out, touching my shoulder briefly then let his hand fall.

"Seriously, it's a good thing. You are more real and grounded than them. What you went through in life has had an impact on you. You think differently, and you're unpredictable. I never know what you'll say or do next. And I like that.

"Most girls I know tend to care more about fashion and make up than what goes on in the real world. They can be shallow and superficial at times and that drives me nuts."

The corners of his mouth tugged upward and his eyes twinkled, making him irresistible. Could he get any more good-looking than this?

I felt my shoulders relax, the tension in my neck gradually disappearing. I lightly punched him in the shoulder. "You really had me scared for a minute there you know?"

He laughed, cringing in mock pain. "Ow!" He shook his head. "I just can't imagine hearing absolutely nothing. You see, even on a quiet day, there is always an undercurrent of sound somewhere." He thought about it, his eyes searching far away in his mind.

I snapped my fingers as an idea came to mind. "Maybe you can..." I put my fingers on my lip as I considered it. "Pick a day like Saturday or Sunday when you don't have much going on. Wear earplugs for that whole day." I smiled at the idea of him wearing earplugs, yelling at his family, telling them to speak up or turning up the television.

His eyebrows inched toward his hairline. "Hey. That's not a bad idea. At least I don't have to hear my parents nag at me."

He seemed thrilled at that thought, fascinated with the concept.

I liked the idea of him walking a mile in my shoes, but I wondered if it would be too much for him to handle. "I gotta warn you though. You may offend some people here and there. There will be times when they will try to get your attention and if you don't respond, they'll get mad at you. Trust me."

He smiled. "S'okay, thanks for the tip. I'll try to keep that in mind."

"Try to keep the earplugs in for most of the day if you can. You will be tempted to take them out at times. I really want you to experience what it's like for me—no cheating allowed."

CHAPTER 15

Surprise

The sun was setting behind the trees, producing fluffy streaks of lavender and orange hued clouds. A group of birds fluttered across the deepening sky, their bodies a dark silhouette against the brilliant backdrop. They swooped gracefully, fluttering their wings occasionally, floating carefree. High above, the sky darkened to a deep cobalt blue. A few stars were barely visible, determined to shine.

I pulled my gaze away from the dramatic sunset long enough to ask him why he insisted on going for a walk. "All right, are you going to tell me what you have up your sleeve yet?"

He tugged at my hand, pulling me across the bridge. The water beneath it seemed to be filled with the liquid hues of the sky. It was mesmerizing. The ripples twisted and twirled the orange, purple, and blue into an abstract painting.

"Oh come on! Not even a hint?" I narrowed my eyes to a slit, insanely curious. He had been secretive for most of the day as if he was plotting something.

He looked at me with a delicious, sly smile. The corners of his lips curled suggestively upward. "Don't worry, you'll see in a minute or two."

We walked side by side in silence, enjoying the stunning scenery before us. I could feel giddy laughter bubbling in my chest, desperately wanting to escape. "Oh! Look at the fireflies! They're everywhere!"

Little orbs of blinking lights appeared to come alive as soon as the sun faded. The bushes twinkled with tiny flashes as if they were sending Morse code to one another.

It felt so magical and childlike. It seemed as if we were being treated to a special display, courtesy of the forest.

I let go of his hand and strolled toward them, skipping a little, and raised my hands in hope of catching one of their lovely glows. I tried to follow one but found their path to be utterly unpredictable. It was hard when they were lit in one spot only to discover they had already flitted to another patch of leaves.

"Ha! I feel like a little kid again!"

Just as I said this, I cupped my hands on a leafy plant and slowly lifted it toward my eyes. I peeked in between my thumbs and sure enough, there was a glow within in it.

"Whadda ya know? I got one!" I didn't have to turn around for I already felt his presence behind me, his warm body so close to me. His hands cupped mine as he rested his chin on my shoulder to peer in. His hands were so warm, they almost seemed too hot against mine.

"Heh! You did! You must be a natural at catching them."

As he spoke, I could swear my heart stopped ever so briefly. I was totally captivated by his husky voice and tender hands.

"Well I had a lot of practice. My brother and I would often go out into the fields by the woods as soon as the sun set, armed with butterfly nets and jars. I used to imagine chipmunks carrying a little lantern that was lit by fireflies. "I smiled at that memory, so free and happy, simply enjoying the magic of a warm evening.

It was becoming uncomfortably dark as the night sky deepened. I opened my hands and watched as the tiny flashes of light disappear. Ethan lifted his arm over my head, grasping my hands together and lifting them to his lips, giving them a soft kiss.

Perhaps he sensed my sudden nervousness at the darkness, because he became more reassuring. "Come on, it's getting a bit too dark here to even see each other."

He was right, I could no longer lip-read him with ease. It was getting harder by the minute to understand what he was saying. I was starting to feel helpless. It was difficult enough not being able to hear my surroundings, being shrouded in the darkness with virtually no visual clues made me feel very vulnerable.

The warmth of his hand made a huge difference in my feeling safe in such a dark area. We walked for a few minutes while I stayed close to his side, feeling ridiculously spooked.

Thankfully, I could see a faint glow of light ahead of me. The gravel pathway crunched beneath my feet as we strolled toward it.

The lights became stronger the closer we got to it, peeking through the tall dark trees. The path curved gently to the left and, as we moved past the trees that obscured my vision, I gasped in awe.

It was stunning, far more enchanting than the lovely fireflies we had seen a few minutes ago. Standing in front of me was the beach house, lit up as brightly as a Christmas tree.

The lights dotted the edge of the roof and swirled around the posts on either side of the wooden porch. I could see that inside more lights glowed softly.

Ethan was holding both of my hands to his chest, watching me as pure delight filled me. I was almost speechless. It was simply beautiful.

"So? What do you think?" he tilted his head slightly, waiting for my response.

Nearly breathless, I said, "I'm in awe. It's beautiful. Did you do this?"

He smiled and tugged me toward the door. "Wait 'til you come inside."

As we crossed the threshold, I could hear jazzy music playing in the background. My eyes roamed around the room, taking in every inch. It was a simple wooden beach house, right out of a Pottery Barn catalog, with bleached wooden floors and walls, and large beams along the ceiling.

He had lights everywhere. There was a string of glowing orbs across the fireplace mantel, woven through a grapevine wreath above it. A hurricane vase on the table was filled to the brim with lights.

I was rooted to the spot, delighted by the scene in front of me. It was magnificent. Seeing my reaction, Ethan tilted his head. "So? What do you think? Like it?"

I blinked. "Like it?" I walked in, touching the lights gently. "I love it! It's like a dream come true."

I turned to look at him, my hand on my chest. "How did you know I would love this?"

He laughed quietly and reached out to me, taking a few steps my way. "I just knew. It seemed like something that you would do. It's you," he said as he grasped my hand once again.

I took another look around the room, admiring the beauty of so many lights, loving their soft glow.

He led me to a spot by the far wall, past the table to a clear spot where a wooden floor gleamed, reflecting the lights in its surface. "Come on, let's dance."

As Michael Buble's voice floated through the room, he gathered me into his arms, gently swaying to the rhythm. It was a glorious moment, so stunningly perfect. I sighed, happy that it wasn't a dream from which I was about to wake up.

As I listened to the melody of the song, I leaned into his chest, feeling the softness of his shirt on my cheek. We spun slowly, and I gazed at the room, amazed at his resourcefulness and desire to please me.

It blew me away, how much work he'd put into all of this. There was so much love in this room it was almost unbearable.

I closed my eyes, loving his warmth against me, feeling so safe in his arms. It seemed so right.

We danced for several minutes. After a while I lost track of the time, simply enjoying the moment. When the last song faded away, we reluctantly pulled ourselves apart. He gently kissed my forehead, lips barely touching, like a feather dancing across my skin.

Looking up, I saw that his cheeks seemed slightly flushed. Before I could say anything, he stopped and tugged me toward the fireplace. In front of it, stood a small, cream-colored wooden table. On top of it was a Scrabble game. There were two glasses filled with a sparkling, bubbly liquid and floating raspberries. I arched my eyebrows at him, glancing at the glasses.

"Try it," he said as he leaned down to light the fireplace and placed the lighter under the twigs. I inhaled the warm scent of burning wood as it began to crackle and was comforted by it. Suspiciously, I brought the glass to my lips and tasted it. It was delicious. "Aha. Sparkling Perrier, with a hint of raspberry flavor. For a minute there, I thought it was wine."

He chuckled, looking my way.

I stared at him as the fire blossomed, casting a golden glow on his features. The flickering light danced in his eyes. He looked like a bronze warrior. My breath caught in my throat for a moment.

I sat down on a large pillow on the floor at the end of the table, with the warm fire on my right side.

He scooted over to his side and fiddled with the board game. "Okay, you ready to play?"

"Sure!" I grabbed a tile from the bag, looked at the letter. "It's the letter A."

He placed his hand in the bag, drew out a tile, glanced at it "L," he said. "You go first."

We both drew seven tiles from the bag and tried to produce a decent word from our selections. Pleased, I came up with the word, "J-E-W-E-L."

"Nice one Jess. Well, let's see that's fifteen points. Double it, which comes to a total of thirty points. Wow, that's a great start!"

After a few minutes of thinking, his word turned out to be, "E-Y-E."

I narrowed my eyes at him. "That's it?"

"Yep," he said smugly, already rearranging the letters in the place holder.

"Hmph. Let's see what I can do here." I frowned, staring at the letters in front of me. "It's not much, but it's all I can do for now. G-A-T-E."

"That's good." He stared at his letters.

As he thought about his next word, I focused on the song playing in the background. I smiled as I recognized the lyrics and its seductive beat. "I've got you under my skin." It was one of my favorite songs.

Ethan looked my way as he placed the letters on the board. His features softened. He gazed at me and softly sighed almost like a cat's purr.

Puzzled, I asked, "What?"

His smile grew wider, bringing a sense of warmth to his handsome face. "Let me guess. This is one of your favorite songs?"

"Oh yes. I love the beat and its seductive mood." I said still listening to it.

He grinned. "I can tell. It really shows on your face."

My face must've flushed.

He quickly added, "Don't worry. You look even more beautiful when you're this happy."

I could feel the heat rising in my cheeks and there was nothing I could do to stop it. I glanced down to avoid his eyes and that's when I noticed his next word, "L-O-V-E."

"So..." He broke into my thoughts, "How did you get hooked on jazz?"

"Oh." I thought back. "Actually it was my grandpa who was interested in it. Whenever we visited him, he always had jazz playing on the CD player. He loved it. I guess I grew to enjoy it too. I can still remember the day I asked him who was singing. He showed me a CD cover with Michael Buble on it. I knew he was too young to be a part of Grampa's generation and Grandpa said that he was actually a part of my generation. I was thrilled. I became even more excited when I found out Michael was Canadian!

"I became hooked, knowing that I'd found a singer younger than Grandpa, you know, even though it was okay to listen to his type of music. Michael's music is so intense. It's like a story unraveling. I can't explain it, but his songs help clear my mind. My worries just disappear."

Ethan drew his knees to his chin, arms wrapped around them. "You know it suits you right?"

"I can't help it. I love his voice."

Feeling a bit too warm from the fire, I moved toward the coach. I noticed that Ethan moved away as well.

We locked gazes. I stared at him, loving how the shadows of the fire danced across his features.

After a minute, he broke my silent adoration. "Okay, it's your turn."

A little hazy, I looked at down the letters. Wow, I thought, feeling a bit too warm.

I tried hard to focus but all I could come up was, "F-A-L-L." *Huh. Could that be a hidden meaning that I'm falling for him?*

He didn't even blink as I placed the letters on the board. "Okay, so that comes to..." he muttered. "All righty, here we go." He plunked down the letters "O-U" in front of "Y" to complete the word, "You."

I looked at the board more closely, recognizing a pattern. He had placed several specific words on it, hardly random choices. My eyes widened as it dawned on me.

"Ethan!"

He feigned innocence, his shoulders shrugging, his eyes laughing. "What?"

"What do you mean, 'What?'" I pointed at the board. "Eye. Love. You."

He shifted closer to me, reached for my left hand, and curled his fingers through mine. "Oh, is that what it says? I didn't even notice."

I just about melted on the spot and desperately held back a groan. I leaned against him, simply absorbing the heat from the fire and his body at the same time.

With his free hand, he pushed a lock of hair away from my forehead, softly kissing the bare skin. His lips slid down underneath my jaw, just behind my ear and I closed my eyes feeling the gentleness of his lips. He continued his trail of kisses, down to my eyes, tip of my nose.

I barely breathed, feeling more dizzy after each kiss. He felt so soft and smelled absolutely delectable.

Finally, his lips touched mine. It was feather light at first. I could feel electric shocks shooting down to my toes.

I pressed against his mouth, savoring his taste. My right hand was on his chest, gripping his shirt and pulling him closer. It was electrifying, the kisses going deeper and deeper as if we couldn't get enough.

Never have I felt so alive.

The room seemed to spin.

Gasping, we broke apart, resting our foreheads together, taking a moment to gather our wits and, of course, our breath.

I could feel his hands on either side of my face, cradling me, occasionally stroking my hair.

After a moment, he pulled away. Looking into his eyes sent a jolt straight into my heart.

"Jess, you okay?" He said, reaching for a stray lock of my hair and tucking it behind my ear.

"Hmm? Oh, of course," I said, floating on a cloud. "All I can say is wow. That was perfect. Everything was perfect tonight."

He laughed and pulled me into a loving embrace as we watched the fire.

CHAPTER 16

Leaves of Three

I was putting the final strokes of Passion Orange polish on my toes when Mom called out from behind me. "Jessie, are you sure you got everything? Did you remember to pack your bathing suit and towels?"

I rolled my eyes skyward and sighed. "Yes, Mom. And my toothbrush. And my PJs."

She brought out my duffel bag, dropped it onto the porch beside me with a heavy thunk, then straightened up as she had another thought. "Oh! Hearing aid batteries!"

"Yep, already packed," I said as I gingerly slid my flip-flops over my toes.

I looked up and could see that she was going to keep talking. "Mom. Would you stop fussing over me already?"

She pointed down the driveway, grinned nervously, and waved. "Actually, it's too late. They're here."

"Oops! I should give this to you," I said as I got up from the porch steps and gave her the nail polish.

I smiled as they pulled up alongside the house and I could see Ethan waving back.

Ethan was nearly out of the car before it came to a complete stop.

"Hey! Ready for the cottage?" he asked as Mom stepped down from the porch and strode over to his parents, probably to exchange ground rules.

I could see them casting a glance our way as we hugged.

He looked over his shoulder, saw them watching us, and snorted back a laugh. "Not very trusting parents, eh?" He bent down and picked up my bag with a grunt. "Geez, what did you pack?"

"Quit your griping, it's not that heavy." As I watched him carry it to the trunk, I admired the light green polo he wore with eggplant purple plaid shorts streaked with mint green. He looked ready for a beach party and it suited him well.

As he dumped the bag in the trunk, I walked over to the car and leaned against it, waiting impatiently for Mom to finish her chat with Ethan's mother.

Finally, they came to an end and gave each other a knowing smile. She turned around and pulled me into a loving bear hug.

"Have a good time honey!" she said as she brushed a lock of hair out of my eyes.

"I will. It's only for a few days."

We broke apart and I slid into the seat beside Ethan.

"Sorry about that," I said as I pulled on the seatbelt.

Ethan's Dad turned around to face us. "So. Are you ready for an adventure?"

Ethan nodded as his father chuckled softly and started the car. "Yep."

After a few minutes of driving through the country and into the city, we made our way onto the 401, slowly merging into an already packed crowd trying to escape for the long weekend.

"Hmph. Looks like everyone else has gotten the same idea as us," remarked Ethan as he glanced out the window.

"Speaking of which, where exactly are we going?" I asked.

"Ah. That would be deep in the woods of Muskoka. We'll probably arrive by suppertime if we're lucky."

He looked up at the sky. "I just hope it doesn't rain. The forecast was calling for thunderstorms later today. This muggy weather is perfect for it."

"Crap. I really don't like storms especially so soon after—you know..." I swallowed my fear as I recalled the tornado that had struck the school a few months ago.

"Hmm?" he said distractedly. "Oh, yeah. I forgot about that."

"You forgot?" I said, somewhat surprised. "How do you forget something like that?"

"You know me. I can be a bit of a scatterbrain."

I squirmed in my seat uncomfortably. "Uh huh. No kidding. So, can we change the subject?"

He grinned at me and reached out to grab my hand. "Heh. Sure."

"Can you teach me sign language?" he asked, curiosity etched on his face.

"Of course! Although Mom knows far more words than I do since she's the one that does all the signing." I searched through my mind for simple signs that he could learn easily. Then I glanced toward the front of the car where his parents sat and got an idea of where to start. "Okay. Let's try this one." I brought up my hand, fingers outstretched with my thumb sticking out to the side. I touched the side of my chin with my thumb, fingers pointed upward. "This is the sign for mother."

Then I moved my hand higher up on my face and tapped my thumb on the side of my temple. "This one is for father."

I saw his Mom turn around in her seat to watch us. She wore a broad smile. I could see his father glancing in the rear mirror to view his progress.

I watched him raise his hand to form the sign father and reached out to correct the positioning. "Good! You've got the hang of it! Now, try this one." I hooked both of my index fingers together to form a cross that fit together like a puzzle, knuckles facing in opposite direction. "This one symbolizes friends or friendship."

It took Ethan a minute to grasp it. "This is so cool," he enthused, clearly enjoying learning how to communicate despite his clumsy attempts at first.

"Here's an easy one." I opened my palm, placed it a few inches away from my chest and mimicked circular motions. "It means please. Just think of the motions that you use to wash the car. If you want to change it to the word sorry, simply close your hand and make a fist and continue the same process."

He looked down at himself and tried to copy my signs.

"Okay. Now, try this one." I demonstrated the sign for thank you as I brought my open hand toward my chin, the tips of my fingers touching my lips and then down again in a brisk motion.

"Wow. That's awesome," he muttered as he worked on the different gestures.

We continued trying all sorts of words that he could sign, the trees blurring in the background behind him. The busy city was no longer evident as the landscape changed to dense woods and rocky hills, large stones jutting out on either side of the highway.

I occasionally spotted the odd Innushuk statue neatly stacked on top of the rocky hills as well as the infamous, "I am Canadian," slogan etched across the surface of the rocks along the side of the road.

Glancing upward, I noticed that the sky had darkened considerably and the window in front was just starting to show wet splatter marks. The drops grew in intensity as we approached the storm, forcing the windshield wipers to sweep across the surface at a faster pace.

I could feel the fear inside me growing to an uncomfortable level.

Ethan pulled my hand to his chest and held it there.

The rain thundered loudly on the roof of the car and at one point, we slowed down to a crawl due to the fierce wall of rain that acted like a barricade.

Finally, the sky gradually became lighter and the intensity of the downpour eased back to a gentle drizzle.

Then there was a sudden burst of light as the sun broke through the clouds.

Katie gasped in delight, turned around, and pointed her finger at the window. "Guys? Do you see this?"

Ethan and I craned forward. We all stared at the majestic rainbow in awe, displayed in a full arc across a dark blue sky.

"Ha! Would ya look at that! The end of the rainbow marks where we are going!" said his dad, looking pleased as punch.

He was right. We arrived in that area within thirty minutes. The car rumbled down a long and winding gravel road, with thick trees on either side, forming natural walls.

We made our way slowly toward the cottage, the tires crunching loudly on the crushed stones.

As we approached the clearing, I could see a simple and rustic log cabin ahead of me, the lower half covered with a mosaic of large flat stones.

After stumbling out of the car a bit stiffly from the long drive, I stretched out my arms to loosen the knots in my shoulders.

Ethan went to the trunk and gathered our bags. I joined him as he ambled toward the cottage.

"Finally! Too bad everything is still a bit wet, eh?" he said as he stretched out his arms and looked around, the water still dripping off the leaves. The air smelled like wet cedar and musty birch trees.

My toes were already getting damp as I walked toward the stairs.

When his dad reached out and pulled open the screened door to unlock the main door its hinges protested loudly. He went inside, letting it slam shut behind him with a bang, and turned on the lights. "Okay, come on in folks!"

Ethan tilted his head toward the door, his hands full of our bags. "After you."

"Hmm? Oh thanks." I pulled on the handle and held the door open to let him and his Mom through.

"Thanks, Jessie," she said with a kind smile as she went by me.

The interior of the cottage was splendid and utterly cozy. It was very much like a ski chalet with a high ceiling and exposed wooden beams. Off to my left was a towering stone chimney. Directly in front of me were expansive windows that showed off a boardwalk leading toward the beach. To my right, were the kitchen and a hallway leading to smaller rooms.

The furniture was elegant in its simplicity, made out of strong wooden logs. Stacked on top were Hudson Bay blankets and pillows, a perfect fit with the natural theme.

Ethan dumped our bags in the rooms at the back while I took in the scenery. It was breathtaking.

He appeared at my side, grinning. "Jessie? Shall I show you to your room?"

"Oh, sure." We went down the hallway as he showed me where the bathroom was located, past his room on the left side and directed me to my room on the right.

"This is our guest room. If there's anything you need, just let us know okay?" He waved his hand into the room, gesturing me inside. A wooden log bed stood in the center with a long dresser off to the side with a small lamp on top.

On the bed lay a colorful quilt. I leaned in closer to admire it, running my fingers over the patterns.

He leaned casually against the doorway. "Grandma Rose made that quilt."

"Really? Oh wow. It's amazing." I turned to face him, suddenly feeling like a stranger in unfamiliar surroundings. "This place is charming. It's funny though, it reminds me of Montana."

He nodded. "It does look like one of their log cabins, doesn't it?" Reaching out to me, he added, "Come on, let's go down to the beach while Mom and Dad unpack."

"Don't they need help?"

"Actually, Mom is quite fussy around the kitchen and prefers to get everything organized on her own. It's easier if we stay out of the way for now. We can help do the dishes after supper as consolation."

He pulled me gently out the back door through the living room, onto a well-worn sandy path leading toward the boardwalk.

"Would you believe that Dad built this walkway?"

"Seriously? It's great."

"We wanted to make it easier for Grandma Rose to go down to the beach. The sand is a bit hard for her to walk on sometimes." He pointed toward the beach, the wind gently tousling his hair. "Make sure you wear something on your feet though. You could get splinters along here."

I looked up as a seagull swooped overhead. "Ah, good point."

The air was fresh and cool, still moist after the storm.

I could see the ominous clouds receding off to the side of the horizon, revealing a luminous blue sky and smooth waters. There were several white seagulls bobbing up and down on the water in the distance.

We strolled casually along the beach, holding hands, simply enjoying the peaceful atmosphere.

Two butterflies flitted in front of us, hovering just above the water, dancing and twirling around each other in a private tango. They seemed to mirror my thoughts, full of happiness and joy.

I bent down to take off my flip-flops and discovered a large gray feather nearby. Delighted, I picked it up.

"Look at the size of this feather!"

He laughed as I brushed his face with its soft edge.

"It's from one of the Canada Geese we have around here. They love this spot, they're usually around in the evening or in the morning."

It was getting cooler. Goose bumps formed on my arms.

Ethan briskly rubbed his hands on my arms, pulling me into his warm embrace. "Getting a bit cold?"

We snuggled together, enjoying the moment.

A tantalizing aroma drifted in our direction. "Mmm, do you smell that? It's probably our supper." Ethan remarked. He lifted his head and gazed in the direction of the cottage.

I inhaled. "Oh, yeah. It smells good."

Invigorated by the delicious aroma, we turned around and walked back, just in time for dinner.

Afterwards, I pulled on a pair of warm sweatpants and hoodie and switched to sneakers.

As I approached the kitchen counter, Ethan pushed a frothy cup of hot chocolate toward me. His other hand held a bag of poufy marshmallows and bucket of kindling.

"Careful. Mom put a special ingredient in it to give it that extra zing. Namely, it has quite a bit of a kick."

I gingerly took a sip. At first, it tasted of rich and strong chocolate, then after a few seconds my tongue began to sizzle. My mouth felt like it was on fire.

I sucked in some air to cool down my tongue. "Whoo! It sure does have that kick! Gasp!"

"That'll keep you warm eh?"

"Holy smokes, yeah." I looked down at the stack of items he was holding. "Anything you want me to carry?"

"Actually, yeah. Can you grab that flashlight from the counter?" He nodded his head in the direction of the table.

I snatched it up and we began our march down the boardwalk.

Off to the left side at the end of the path was a well-used fire pit, sheltered by a small sand dune and scrawny trees. There were several large logs lying on their sides around the fire pit, forming a natural bench.

As we unloaded everything beside the benches, Ethan's father began stacking the kindling and wood into a pile. He flicked his lighter at the base, waiting for it to flare to life.

The fire flourished into a crackling roar, filling the air with a smoky scent.

Ethan and I began to add marshmallows to the prongs of the roasting forks and handed them out to his parents. As they placed their treats over the flames, we tacked on ours and swung them into the blaze.

We gleefully munched on our sticky marshmallows as the sun set, providing us with a display of pink and orange streaks.

I glanced out toward the lake and noticed that it was eerily calm, almost as smooth as glass. I could hear the gentle sloshes of water as it lapped the edges of the shore.

As we admired the warm fire, we chatted back and forth about Ethan growing up here, how he used to swim butt-naked in the lake as a toddler. He blushed at his mother's revelations. "Aw! Mom!"

Without warning, there was a burst of light behind us and sudden popping sounds. "What was that?"

I turned around to see what was going on and was pleasantly surprised to discover that it was a display of fireworks.

"Ah. That must be our neighbors. They often celebrate the holidays with fireworks," Ethan said. His face lit up in shades of green and red from the glow of the pyrotechnics.

They were impressive as they rose high up in the night sky and burst into sparkling blossoms, their reflections shimmering on the water.

After the fireworks display was over, Ethan's parents stood up and stretched. "Well, we really should be getting back. Watch out for the bears and don't forget to put out the fire."

Alarmed, I turned around and said. "Bears? What bears?"

"Don't worry, as long as we make plenty of noise, they will stay away from us."

Not exactly reassured, I scooted closer to him, my eyes darting around. "Have you ever had bears around here?"

He chuckled. "As a matter of fact, we did. Grandpa saw him one night as it went right up to the screen door and stood on its hind legs to peer in. He said it was the spookiest thing he had ever seen as the two of them faced each other, separated only by the door."

I prodded him. "Uh huh. Then what happened?"

"He grabbed a couple of pots and pans and banged them together as loudly as possible. It worked. The bear ran away, terrified of the noise."

Trying to take my mind off the bear, I turned around to gaze at the glittering night sky.

"Too bad that there isn't a full moon tonight. It would've been a nice touch."

"Hmm, yeah but you wouldn't have been able to see the fireworks as well though. Nor the stars in the night sky, like the Big Dipper up there." He grasped my hand and pulled it upward to point out the stars.

"Where?" I asked as I looked up, trying to find it.

"See the points of the handle and pot up there? It looks like it's tipping it."

I could feel the warmth of his other hand on my shoulder and his face near my cheek as he spoke.

"Oh, yeah. I see it now. That's awesome!"

I swiveled back to the fire to get warm again as it was getting really cold.

His voice broke my thoughts. "Jessie? How do you say I love you?"

I blinked, momentarily confused, then recalled our earlier session of learning sign language.

I gently gripped his hand, tucked two of his middle fingers downwards into his palm, leaving the two outer fingers pointing upward like a bull's horn with his thumb out sideways like a hitchhiker's.

"That is cool!" he mused as his looked as his hand, his eyes twinkling in the glow of the fire.

I shivered from the effects of the cool evening. He pulled me into a warm embrace as both of us faced the fire, his arms wrapped around me like a cozy blanket. I snuggled deeper into his arms as he rested his chin on my shoulder.

Suddenly Ethan sat up a little straighter, jerking his head upward in concentration. "Did you hear that?"

I froze as a chill of fear raced down my spine. "No. What? What do you hear?"

He titled his head as he listened intently. "There it is again."

"What?"

"The wolves. They're howling in the distance. It's spooky."

I strained to hear them but heard nothing, although I was getting more paranoid by the minute.

"No. I can't hear them. It's beyond the range of my hearing aids." I felt a stab of shame and intense sadness at not being able to hear those sounds and cursed my hearing loss right then. I would've loved to share that moment with him.

"Oh, I'm so sorry, Jessie. I didn't realize..." He pulled me into a hug as he said this.

After a while, the embers began to die down to a gentle glow, too subtle to provide much warmth anymore.

Ethan grabbed a bucket of water that sat nearby and doused the dim fire, causing it to sizzle and sputter.

We grabbed the flashlight and started heading back to the cottage.

I was so focused on watching where I was going that I didn't even noticed that Ethan was not behind me.

"Ethan? Where are you?"

I swung my flashlight wildly from side to side, searching for him.

"Ethan! Stop it!"

Suddenly I felt a push from behind and a loud, "Gotcha!"

I screamed and nearly jumped several feet in the air like a scared cat.

My heart was thumping nonstop and my hands shook like crazy. "Ethan! You scared the crap out of me!" I smacked him on the shoulder for good measure.

His laughter echoed down the boardwalk as we stepped into the warm cottage.

c⁓c⁓

I awoke to a beautiful morning. The sunshine streamed cheerfully through the bedroom window. I inhaled the delicious scent of coffee and cinnamon. My mouth watered as I made my way toward the kitchen.

"Morning, sleepyhead. Hungry?" inquired Katie, smiling mischievously. I could see where Ethan got his playful nature. She lifted a plate of cinnamon buns in my direction. "Would you like one?"

"Mmm...thanks! Oh! These are great!" I said as the sweet and sticky cinnamon melted in my mouth.

"Just finished making them. Did you want anything to drink? Coffee...Tea...Juice?"

"Tea would be nice."

"Coming right up!"

I looked around. Ethan's father was at the kitchen table eating. "Morning!" he said cheerfully.

"Where's Ethan?"

"Probably sound asleep. Give him a few more minutes. The aroma is bound to wake him up." He grinned as he said this.

I grinned back at him as I nodded.

"Jessie? Here's your tea." She slid a steaming cup in my direction.

"Oh thanks," I said and added a little bit of sugar. "You know what? I'm going to go down to the beach for a few minutes."

I strolled down the boardwalk and sat on the edge, the cup of tea beside me as I finished off the last bit of the bun, licking my fingers.

It was foggy across the water and along the beach, creating a completely different landscape than yesterday. The mist floated lazily across the water, slowly rising and disappearing as the day became warmer.

I could see faint shadows along the edge of the shoreline and then heard the sounds of honking, and realized that they were coming from the Canada Geese that Ethan had mentioned yesterday.

It was a peaceful morning and had a calming effect on me. I inhaled deeply, taking in the gentle energy.

"Boo!" Ethan shouted me from behind, grabbing my shoulders.

I flinched and my heart thumped wildly, galloping out of control. "Ethan! You almost gave me a heart attack!"

"Sorry. I couldn't resist," he said, grinning like the cat that had swallowed the canary.

I narrowed my eyes at him. "You know there's a saying 'What goes around, comes around.' I wouldn't be surprised if fate or karma played a trick on you."

He stuck his tongue out. "We'll see."

After a few minutes of contemplation, he held up his hand in the form of "I love you."

"You did it!" I repeated the gesture to him, our silent affection for each other.

"Mom and Dad are going raspberry picking later on. Wanna come?"

"Sounds yummy, sure!"

We spent a few more minutes watching the fog evaporate, revealing a sparkling lake and dozens of Canada Geese swimming on the surface, flapping their wings.

Afterwards, we went back to the cottage, got dressed and, armed with empty fruit boxes, we walked down the winding pathway into the woods.

We reached a clearing filled with an abundance of raspberry bushes, sitting on top of a rocky hill. I stretched out my arms, plucking the ripe and lush pink berries. I tucked a couple in mouth, savoring the rich sweetness.

My basket quickly grew full so I strolled back toward Ethan whose basket was clearly only half-full. It was evident that he was eating them rather than collecting them.

Looking down, I realized where he was standing.

"Ethan? I have a question for you."

"Uh huh," he said, partially distracted as he popped another raspberry in his mouth.

"Are you familiar with the phrase 'Leaves of three, leave them be?'"

Puzzled, he stopped midway and looked at me. "I have no idea. Why?"

"Well...It's a reference to Poison Ivy." I pointed at his feet. "You're standing in it."

Alarmed, he twirled around.

"Gah!" He leapt straight up and threw his box of berries in the air. I caught it midair as he hopped around wildly, leaping out of the bushes and back on to the pathway.

He shuddered. "Ugh."

I had tears running down my face from laughing so hard.

"Now that's impressive. What do you call it? The Poison Ivy Jig?" I asked as I swiped at my wet cheeks.

His scowl turned into a shy chuckle as he heard my laughter.

I gingerly stepped through the hillside and stopped in my tracks as something glinted near Ethan's feet.

I gestured in his direction. "Ethan, what's that on the ground beside you? It's sparkling."

Alarm flashed across his face again then eased away as he bent down to examine it curiously.

I wondered if it was another fossil. We had spotted many of them along the trail.

I put down the baskets and leaned in closer. He held it up to the sun. It was a crystallized stone, creamy white with glittering facets. The end of the stone was sheared off, revealing rows of dazzling bits of quartz. He placed it in the palm of my hand.

"They look like diamonds," I said breathlessly as I stared at it in admiration.

He closed his hand over mine. "From my heart to yours, here's a diamond for you to keep."

I tucked the stone into my pocket, feeling its warmth against my body. We picked up our respective boxes and sauntered down the path, hand in hand.

We spent the rest of the weekend eating raspberry pie, swimming in the brisk water of the lake and generally relaxing by the fire in the cool evenings.

Ethan and I sat on the porch swing at home before parting ways, his arm draped across my shoulders for comfort. I held the glittering stone in my hand, watching it twinkle as he said goodbye to me. "All you have to do is look at this and remember."

My heart ached as the car slowly proceeded down the lane. I saw him turn around and sign, 'I love you' with his hand.

CHAPTER 17

Happy Birthday

Summer went by much too quickly for me. I was reluctant to go back to school, especially after spending so much time with Ethan. He was the highlight of my life and I felt very lucky to have him with me. It tore my heart to be apart from him. It was even more painful since we went to separate schools and would see less of each other during the school year. I took every opportunity to see him, more so on the weekends. This weekend in particular was my birthday and I was thrilled to spend it with him.

He bounced eagerly on his feet. "Well? You going to open it?" he said as he watched me pull the ribbon off my gift.

I was a little suspicious at his enthusiasm and wondered what he was up to now, so I deliberately moved slower, trying to drive him crazy. And it was working. I smiled in response. "I'm going as fast as I can!" I peeled back the bright pink wrapping paper and stood frozen to the spot.

I stared at the book in shock, utterly speechless. Ethan laughed as soon as he saw my reaction. "Ha! I knew it!" He elbowed me in the ribs. "Go on, open it." Puzzled, I flipped open the cover.

I looked at him and them back down again at *Harry Potter and the Philosopher's Stone*, not believing it. "H—How?" I began, stammering. "How is this possible?"

My fingers traced the signature, following the curves as it swooped up and down elegantly. *Happy Birthday, Jessie, J.K. Rowling.*

It was a limited edition book, one of the few hundred from the original run. To me it felt like I was holding the Holy Grail in my hands. I stared at it in mute shock.

"Hmm? Oh that...we met at a charity fundraiser a while ago and I mentioned to her that I was looking for a birthday gift for you. She had this one and offered to autograph it for me," he remarked casually, as if it was no big deal,

I was awestruck that he had actually met her. She was literally my hero. I loved her books and greatly admired her imagination and her deeply-creative, rich stories.

Trying not to cry, I gave him a heartfelt hug. "Thank you so much. You have no idea how much this means to me."

I felt his lips on my forehead, kissing gently as he wrapped his arms around me. "My pleasure, Jess. Really, I was just in the right place at the right time. It was as if fate meant for that to happen."

"No kidding. I can't even to tell you how lucky I feel right now." I reluctantly pulled away from his warm embrace and looked into his eyes.

"Ah, but it's not over yet." He smiled, eyes twinkling, reached into his pocket and pulled out a set of keys.

Puzzled I asked, "What could possibly be better than this?" I watched him jangle the keys in his hand, dangling them in front of me.

"I talked it over with my parents and we all agreed to treat you to a mini driving lesson right here in our driveway." His grin became bigger by the minute.

I blinked my eyes, processing this. "Nooo...are you serious?" I said as it dawned on me that he was telling the truth. It took a lot of effort not to jump up and down like a kid. I tried to act as mature as possible, but I was not successful in hiding my joy.

"When can we start? I said, immensely grateful for this opportunity.

"Oh—how about now?" He led me toward a row of cars all gleaming in the sun by the garage. Thankfully these were not the vintage cars nor the insanely expensive ones I had seen his father drive.

The one in front of me was a fairly nondescript navy blue BMW, obviously out of my family's price range, but suited for driving around here.

As he guided me around to the driver's side, his hand on my back, I happened to look up and was surprised to see his parents sitting on the large balcony, overlooking the property, watching everything unfold below them. I waved sheepishly at them and they waved back, clearly enjoying today's activities as they sipped their drinks.

I couldn't help but wonder if they had snuck out to watch my reaction to Ethan's generous gifts.

"Okay, are you ready for a test drive Jess? Now, I have to warn you that a stick shift takes some getting used to," he said as he held the door open, also glancing upward at his parents' amused faces. He did a finger wave toward them and I could have sworn that he winked at them.

"Huh? Wait a minute. Did you say stick shift? As in standard?" I said, suddenly feeling nervous. I slid into the driver's seat and put my hands on the wheel. "How do you know I won't a hit a tree or something?"

He smiled. "Trust me, you won't hit a tree."

Holy Schamoley. The seat was unbelievably comfortable, my butt clearly sinking deeper into the soft cushion. *Now that's luxury.*

Ethan ran around to the other side and jumped into his seat. I adjusted the mirrors and shifted my seat forward so that I could reach the pedals. "Gee, someone has long legs in this family," I muttered, looking toward Ethan for a moment.

He smiled, blushing slightly. "Yeah, that would be me, sorry about that."

Satisfied that everything was within easy reach for me, I said, "Okay, now what?" I stared at the dials on the dashboard. It looked like a James Bond car, everything gleamed as if it was recently polished. It looked expensive. *God, I hope I don't break anything.*

Ethan leaned forward, one hand on the dashboard for balance, the other on his knee. I tried impressively hard not to lean into him. Otherwise I wouldn't be able to stop myself from kissing him.

He pointed down at my feet. "Okay, notice that there are three pedals instead of the usual two."

"Oh yeah, that's a good point. What do I do first?" I asked, slightly apprehensive.

"Before you turn on the engine, you need to step on the clutch and brake, otherwise the car will stall."

I gingerly placed my left foot on the clutch and my right foot on the brake.

He watched me like a hawk. "Ready? Turn the keys but don't take your feet off the pedals yet."

I reached over the steering wheel, fingers on the keys with one eye closed in fear I might snap it in half. I took a deep breath and cranked it over. It purred to life. So far, so good, I thought, relieved for a moment.

"Great! Now shift it into first gear," he said, pointing to the stick, its knob covered by a worn leather surface.

I grunted with effort, not used to this sort of motion.

"Okay, take your foot off the brake and slowly ease your foot off the clutch and step on the gas."

I held my breath as I tried it, my heart pounding as fear suddenly coursed through my body.

Gradually shifting both feet took some getting used to because it felt so strange to me. Unfortunately, I didn't quite time it right and the car shuddered to a sudden stop.

I cringed as it died. "Oops, sorry about that."

"Don't worry about it. It took me a while to get the hang of it. Go ahead and try it again."

I stepped on the pedals, turned the key, and slowly shifted my feet, holding my breath again.

The car rolled forward slowly and I stepped on the gas a little more, elated. "Yes, it worked!"

"Ha! I told you could do it!" He grinned. "Now, the hard part, shifting the gears. Can you feel the change in the engine? It needs to go into second gear. Now, step on the clutch and quickly shift gears."

I balked. "What? Now?" My hand flew to the gearshift. I stepped on the clutch and pulled it back into second gear.

Unfortunately, I didn't do it fast enough and the car lurched to a sudden stop.

"Ack!" I said as the seatbelt tightened across my shoulders. I raised my eyebrows in surprise.

"That's harder than I thought." As I said that, I glanced past Ethan's shoulder and spotted the gardener sitting on his knees, watching us, and laughing quietly, clearly amused.

We didn't go far, hardly past the gates but still, it was a worthwhile experiment.

I tried it again, concentrating with effort, bringing the car to a comfortable speed. The tires crunched on the gravel lane way, as we went through the gates and down the long road.

After spending most of the day with Ethan, it was time to go back home. We reluctantly said our goodbye's as I clutched the book to my chest. As soon as I got home, I made a mad dash to my room, sat down on the bench by the window, and promptly cracked open the book. Parker pounced onto the soft cushions with me and curled up by my feet.

After a period of intense reading, Dad's voice broke through my quiet preoccupation.

"Jessie!" he called up the stairs prompting me to jerk my neck upward.

I got up and looked down the stairs at him. "What?"

"There's a package here for you."

Curious, I ran down the stairs as fast as I could, careful not to fall. I spotted the FedEx package sitting on top of the dining room table.

Breathless, I snatched it up, glancing at the return address and noted that it was from my brother. My eyebrows knitted together as I wondered what it could be. It was thick and soft. I ripped open the package and pulled out a soft fleecy shirt in shades of pink with a letter tucked in between the folds.

I was elated. It felt like the clouds had parted and heaven opened up just for me. I picked up his letter and sat down in awe as I read the note. His timing couldn't have been more perfect. This was like the final piece of the puzzle, clicking into place. After a year of turmoil, it was as if everything was changing for the better, especially now that Ethan was a big part of my life.

Dear Jess, Thought you might like this shirt. I got it especially with you in mind. Let me know if it's warm enough for you! Happy Birthday, with love, your Bro.

I touched it gingerly and brought it to my chest, hugging it. *It's perfect! Perfect for a day like this.* I couldn't believe my luck. I had never told him about what happened to his other shirt.

Thrilled with it, I immediately pulled it on. "Dad! I'm going for a walk in the woods okay? I'm taking Parker with me."

As if on cue, Parker came running down the stairs, meowing when I opened the door. Together, we stepped outside into the bright sunshine.

The trees were lit up with dazzling colors of rich amber and deep reds, like fireworks exploding across the landscape. The ground was covered in a blanket of leaves like a multi-hued quilt.

We strolled past the tall swaying sunflowers, following the worn-out path toward the woods. I sucked in my breath as a Bluebird swooped down and landed on top of the tallest sunflower a few feet away from me, its bright blue feathers glistening in the sun. "Oh wow! It means good luck if I see one! It's beautiful!" I exclaimed as my breath caught in my chest.

We ambled on the path that led us deep into the valley. As we sat on a pile of crunchy leaves, beneath a large tree, its roots cradling me, I looked up and watched the leaves shake in the breeze.

I leaned against the bark, enjoying the warm sun on my face and feeling the gentle breeze flow around me.

I looked down at Parker, stroking his toasty warm fur, and remarked how unusual it had been last year to witness a leaf spiral around the trunk a tree as it floated downwards. He looked up at me, blinking, and seemed to smile at me. As the shadows of the leaves danced across his fur, it glowed in the sun, shimmering with golden sparkles.

Suddenly several leaves fell from three nearby trees, swirling in the exact same pattern as last time. I gasped with delight and laughed. "It was you all along!"

About the Author

Growing up surrounded by a seemingly never ending supply of books provided an ample playground for Jennifer Gibson's imagination. A voracious reader at a young age, she delved into the rich worlds created by talented writers like Madeleine L'Engle, *A Wrinkle in Time*, which planted the seed of her passion for unique adventures. Encouraged by her creative writing teachers, her love for books blossomed into a full grown talent when she became inspired to create an original series based on her life as hard of hearing teenager.

CPSIA information can be obtained at www.ICGtesting.com
Printed in the USA
LVOW132020101012

302329LV00020B/21/P